THE
COMPASSIONATE
TERRORIST

BRIAN GODFREY

Matador
9 Priory Business Park,
Wistow Road, Kibworth Beauchamp,
Leicestershire. LE8 0RX
Tel: 0116 279 2299
Email: books@troubador.co.uk
Web: www.troubador.co.uk/matador
Twitter: @matadorbooks

ISBN 978 1785893 445

British Library Cataloguing in Publication Data.
A catalogue record for this book is available from the British Library.

Printed and bound by CPI Group (UK) Ltd, Croydon, CR0 4YY
Typeset in 11pt Baskerville by Troubador Publishing Ltd, Leicester, UK

Matador is an imprint of Troubador Publishing Ltd

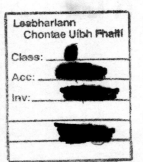

When writing on controversial subjects, it is necessary to discuss with your closest ally the consequences that are relevant. In this case it is my darling wife Pat, with whom I have as a result had some eh, Interested discussions.

After travelling around the world as an expatriate for many years, and meeting so many fantastic people of all races and creeds, I have learnt the art of understanding.

I dedicate this book to my wife, and to all those wonderful people too numerous to mention here.

FOREWORD

1978
RELIGION THE CULPRIT

Many of the Irish, after many years of strife, were tired; they'd had enough of the famine, the hardship, the cold, trying to cultivate a barren land, and the everlasting war with the British; they just moved on to pastures new.

They migrated wherever they could, to make a new life for themselves doing what they knew best, integrating with others hoping to make a better life for their families.

Integration does not always come cheaply in the Promised Land: a smile becomes a frown, a handshake a fist, the good neighbour has misgivings and doubt, the religion and regional accents have a say!

New settlers often become segregated from the locals when starting a new life, and with those who travelled from Ireland at this time, they often felt a barrier. Treated with distrust by the locals, the scepticism was not necessarily of religion, but of their Irish heritage.

Those who travelled far away, from the Troubles, did more often than not make a better life for themselves, but those who stayed at home faced hostilities and civil war.

In 1922, after many years of persecution, and the confrontations that followed, the British and Irish governments agreed a ceasefire with both sides promising to discuss a peace plan, known as the Anglo-Irish Treaty.

The Irish had one intention in mind and that was to form one country, free from British rule; it was to be governed from Dublin (Oireachtas) and democratically elected by the Irish people.

As complex as the situation was at the time, it became even more difficult to solve the problem due to the massive mistrust that the Irish had for the British Government.

Progress in the development of the plan was maintained for a while; a peace plan was in sight, only if the people of Ireland believed it was possible; it seemed that half of them thought it was not!

An agreement was finally reached between the Irish Treaty delegates and the British Government in London in December 1921 but the conditions were fraught with uncertainties and distrust.

A section of the Irish people supported President Éamon de Valera with the majority remaining following Michael Collins, a reputable PIRA general at the time.

But the treaty between the Irish delegation and Westminster was burdened with uncertainties and doubt, and the outcome was almost inevitable.

The pending result could split the Irish people, bringing the country to its knees, hastening the inevitable, a state of war.

The treaty was signed in December 1921, allocating a new state in Ireland named Irish Free State (Saorstat Eireann), this was subject to the right of a six-county region situated in the north of the country, later to be called Ulster, and this would remain under British rule.

The events in this story occur at the end of 1978 and into 1981 at a time when the feelings of distrust between the parties were at their worst.

A ceasefire was agreed during 1976 and lasted a short time, but it lacked integrity and only provided a breathing space for both parties.

PROLOGUE

AN ORDINARY TOWN

Rostrevor is a small town in Northern Ireland situated in close proximity to the border between the North and South of Ireland.

Not much has changed here over the last two hundred years, although the troubles between the British Army and the Provisional Irish Republican Army (PIRA) have left their scar.

The nearby border towns of Warren Point and Newry have seen their share of the conflict and the area has become notorious, mainly because of its precarious border location.

In the true sense of the word the Unionists have regarded this area of Ireland as bandit country.

During the war years with the British it was deemed dangerous to venture into any of the pubs or meeting places as a stranger, and even more so with an English accent.

The finger that points can label an innocent person guilty without recourse, the outcome untenable.

Fear and suspicion between people can jeopardize the lives of any person in the community; it leaves a large heavy grey cloud over everyone.

Troubles between the Unionist North and the Rebel Catholic South have long being a bone of contention, the North wanting to retain their British and Protestant background and the South wanting an independence for the whole of Ireland, not just part of it.

The brutality that has occurred between the two factions, with the North supported by the British Army and the South by the Irish Republican Army, are too numerous and complex to discuss in a single session.

Killings and maimings have been plentiful, but there can be no reason for the taking of a human life, and any such cause cannot be justified. Bobby Sands, the Nationalist, died fighting for better rights for prisoners, and his ultimate sacrifice now seems so futile.

The policy of the PIRA was always to justify the killings and injuries that they were responsible for, but they too had suffered death and tragedies during the bitter fight for freedom.

Those early years of British occupation and the lack of sympathy for their cause, made the Irish bitter; the British needed to be challenged, and the IRA took it on to do this.

The subsequent acts of violence carried out by the IRA during the Troubles; met with supreme counter aggression by the British, with the height of hostilities occurring between 1975 and 1985.

Repeated delays in proposals and failure to maintain promises by the British made the Irish efforts even more determined, the terms of terrorism became desperate, the PIRA could wait no longer.

Aggression and violence between factions without hurting others is only temporary, and it was only a matter of time before innocent people would be killed in the crossfire.

The one thing that people in occupied countries have in common is the ignominious fact that the real people have little to say in their country's destiny.

If the politicians of this world are to be wise, then history must have a say; occupation of a country is only temporary, the reversal is inevitable.

The process may take months, or it may take years, it will nevertheless happen.

If peace was to be achieved in Ireland, it would not come cheaply, with the cost of more fatalities; the impending grief cannot ever be justified.

The situation in 1975 between the North and South of Ireland was in a complex state; the Troubles started to simmer and it looked as if the ceasefire would not last long.

Politically little had changed for nearly fifty years, with the exception of the 1922 treaty, and this did not solve anything.

The North of Ireland remained a part of the United Kingdom; with its people forming the Ulster government, the Unionists strongly allied to Britain.

The majority of Northern Ireland parliamentarians were members of the Ancient Orange order of Orangemen – a secret Masonic-type of society that was founded after William II defeated the Nationalists at the Battle of the Boyne.

The order is sworn to defend the Protestant faith in the face of adversity and is one of the biggest problems that faces the peace process between the North and South of Ireland.

The Protestant religion loses its significance when supported by such a bigoted belief and is the medium that promotes the hate between the Irish people.

The marches that parade through Belfast and the Irish quarter every year on 12th July stir up hatred and revive the terrible memories of the past.

In 1979 there was no simple solution, the majority of British were embedded in the North, and the nationalists in the South. The difference may be insurmountable – only the future will tell.

Early in the twentieth century, the British Prime Minister Lloyd George and his Liberal government were condemned internationally for not stabilizing the situation of unrest that was prevalent in Ireland.

The government finally reacted and passed the Government Act of Ireland and this was supposed to introduce a form of parity.

Due to a turn of events, the situation worsened when the Prime Minister introduced a biased polling strategy, where only Protestants could cast a vote.

Home Rule never took effect in southern Ireland, due to the Irish War of Independence, which resulted in the Anglo-Irish Treaty and the establishment in 1922 of the Irish Free State. However, the institutions set up under this Act for Northern Ireland continued to function until they were suspended by the British parliament in 1972 as a consequence of the Troubles.

Catholics residing in the North of Ireland have found life difficult: the intimidation, the unfair segregation and the bullying.

Most big businesses at this time were managed or owned by Unionists and job allocation always favoured the Protestant.

Catholic tradesmen were treated as second best with the cream of the work going to the Unionists, many out of work, the lucky ones including academics and tradesmen driving taxis for a meagre living.

The large modern roads which were built in the North with funds supplied by the British abruptly came to an end at the border, the larger roads suddenly transcending to small country counterparts.

Small towns both in the North and South of Ireland away from the cities and border towns carried on in their own indomitable way.

Those towns situated in the border corridor between the

North and South did the same although with the difference of one word – fear!

Rostrevor is a town within the commuting area of Belfast, it has natural beauty, close proximity to the famed Mourn Mountains, and should be an ideal place to live!

Serene against a blue sky the mountains sweep into the Lough, walking paths wind between the giant redwood trees that stand so elegantly on the banks of the loch.

These have been utilized over many centuries; the weary feet of travellers passing daily have transformed them into the undulating characteristics of today.

Being no more significant than other villages spread across the Irish countryside, it has notoriety, due to the location, with close proximity to the border.

It is positioned on the banks of Carlingford Lough, in easy commuting distance with the principle towns of Warrenpoint and Newry, both made famous through the notoriety of the Troubles.

The mountains themselves tell of another story, another tale of aggression and might, this time fought long ago between two giants; the scars of that battle remain today.

These two titans bellowing and breathing fire meet on the two opposite peaks on the local mountains, one called Finn McCool stood defiantly on one peak whilst his adversary Cuhulin, the Manx giant, stood on the other.

The two hurled huge rocks savagely at each other from the opposite peaks, the missiles filled the sky and those that fell short of target broke into smithereens, and have lain untouched ever since. The legend, probably biased, has proclaimed Finn the winner, the real truth may never be known.

The rocks can be seen today, strewn across the beautiful County Down landscape, large and small alike remain as a legacy of the battle.

One of the larger sections of rock is called the Cloughmore Stone. It has become a favourite visiting place for tourists.

Many visitors over the years inscribed names on the rock face, some going back year after year to do it over and over again.

Similar to others, this village has not changed its secrets, its character and its troubles in hundreds of years.

All that looks beautiful in life is often not; the town of Rostrevor has a dark side to its beauty, one that is called fear, where a word out of place may arouse suspicion or associating with new or unknown faces may cause misconception.

Even in the sanctuary of the church and the confessional it was necessary to curb the truth. Idle gossip on the street was not tolerated, and the locals knew better, never risking the safety of themselves or their family.

Risks were rarely taken, it was a given; the ordinary people kept their heads down and remained silent for the outside world to see.

Nobody could be trusted, and loose talk was avoided; a rule among the people.

The pubs in any village can provide the best local cultural history, both through general gossip or by the old stained photographs that portray olden times. Many of which hang on the pub walls as a constant reminder of bygone days.

Old men sit on stools at the back of the bar and sip their drinks.

The old folk never seem to change their ways, always the same stools, the same clothes.

Alas, when they do change they die and other old men, on those same stools where others have sat before them, sit now.

Each of these old men has a story to tell; the tales are handed down to the next set of old men to talk about.

That's how legends are made, and men made immortal.

The old men fade away, but their stories do not, and these hold the cultural history of the village.

1

A STEP TOO FAR

AUGUST 1979

An old car with a driver and one passenger drove along the A2 from Warrenpoint heading towards the town of Newry in County Down, Northern Island.

The road was busy and the men were finding it difficult to find a place to stop without causing either an accident or drawing attention to themselves.

Finally they turned into the entrance to Narrow Water Castle on the banks of Carlingford Lough, at a place where the narrow strip opens up to the sea.

"It's a pity it is so near the castle but the bend in the road will be an advantage to us," said the passenger.

The driver was thoughtful, but after a short pause he answered, "To be sure, the soldiers will be concentrating on the bend when the trucks come along that road; their minds will be on other things, especially knowing they have a long working day ahead. It may have been better in hindsight to target the trucks on the return from Newry. Tired after a days work they may be a better target."

The man in the passenger seat challenged. "Maybe and maybe not," he replied. "They may well be tired and they may also be only interested in planning their trip to the pub after their dinner, but that's the way it was agreed at the meeting and that's the way we are going to go!"

The passenger, a man called O'Donnell, strengthened his argument. "Remember, in this direction it is closer to the south side and it will be easier for us to hit them with automatic fire from across the burn when necessary."

O'Donnell continued, "When it happens, the British are expected to respond with a team from Newry immediately they are alerted about the incident, so we expect the second wave to be on the scene in about forty minutes and we can hit them from the south again."

The driver, the smaller of the two men, called McInerny queried the plan. "How do we detonate a second device in the area that the first has blown? That will not work, surely to God."

"The paras will not go directly to the heart of the explosion straight away, but set up the command post close to the first, it is British military tactics, but in any event the second device will be hidden in a place out of range from the first."

His voice continued as if programed, "We anticipate them setting up camp by the gatehouse, the nearest point to the first blast, and those who survived will seek the nearest cover."

O'Donnell seemed to have all the answers and was confident of the plans and when his colleague tried to speak, he held up his hand in a gesture for him to stop.

"You see, my friend, with the river running along the south side and the bend in the road obscuring the view, the soldiers have nowhere else to set up the base after regrouping – other than the gatehouse, and that is where our second device will be, exactly there!"

"So we detonate the small house?"

"Or close to it," answered O'Donnell.

"The trucks are so fucking big, maybe two or three tons or so, we will need a big one, probably three hundred pounds or more for the first truck and a bit more for the second because the house needs to be demolished completely in order to have maximum impact."

O'Donnell was silent but sat looking smugly out at the castle.

He went on speaking as if McInerny did not exist. "Such a bloody pretty place for a killing, but the paras need this, especially as a mark of respect for Bloody Sunday."

"Where will we be?" asked McInerny.

"On the south side, together with detonator and automatics," explained O'Donnell.

"The supreme command will be suitably impressed," said McInerny.

"They fucking will not, because they'll not know a bloody thing until it is all over."

"How do we get away? Because the way I see it the army will have choppers here in about twenty minutes," said McInerny.

"OK, enough, let's hit the bloody road and get things finalized over the next week or so."

They started the car and headed back along the A2 and south towards Omeath in County Louth.

A few days later four men were sitting in a pub close to the ferry terminal in a border town called Omeath.

O'Donnell bought the drinks and his four colleagues sat down at a table away from the main bar.

The table was strategically at the rear of the pub, under an arch at the end of a short passageway.

The men were members of the Irish Republican Army from the South Armagh Brigade; they had assembled to discuss the preparations for the proposed attack on the British at Narrow Water Castle.

"There is something going on at Brigade headquarters, but I don't bloody well know what it is."

"Why?" asked the short fat man with red hair. He sat as a watchman at the end of the table.

Positioned with his back against the window and facing the passage to the bar, he was the 'look out' and would change the conversation the instant anything suspicious was anticipated.

"Because when I spoke to Duggan about our plans he just stared ahead and said, 'Not now, William'. So fuck him; we are doing our thing, and if they don't like it then too fucking bad."

"Is that wise?" McInerny seemed nervous.

"It doesn't fucking matter. We do it and we do it well."

The fourth man then spoke. He was a tall gaunt man in his fifties. "Come on guys, we will do it properly, but this thing is big, and the operation will need to be tested and rehearsed until we are sure it will work without a hitch."

"If we are going to test it, it will need to be a long way from the garda because this big bastard will make one helluva bang!"

26TH AUGUST 1979

A small open-backed van drove along the A2, and pulled in at the castle.

Inside, three men were dressed in dirty blue boiler-suits with the word Water stencilled on their backs.

They stopped the traffic and put Road Up signs in strategic places.

The second man moved further up the road and laid out a Road Narrows sign – they intended to divert the traffic into a single lane.

It was important that the traffic was held from both directions so it would give the two men time to place the bomb-laden milk pallets close to the gatehouse.

"It will be necessary to close both lanes for a short time,"

4

O'Donnell had advised earlier, and the men had prepared Halt signs and these were utilized to hold traffic for a few precious minutes.

The third man removed the large package from the open-backed vehicle and placed this on the back of the truck near to the road where the convoy was to pass.

A second small truck arrived with straw and associated material and the driver used a fork to spread the hay over the back of the truck, and it was driven close to the gatehouse.

Within five minutes they were packing away the tools in the two trucks and had redirected traffic on both lanes.

One of the men returned briefly to the truck on the road and placed an official-looking note that explained to the police that the truck was being moved later on the Monday after much of the holiday traffic had subsided.

The devices that were in position were built to be more powerful than what was first estimated; this was a contingency in case the trucks were heavier than first thought.

A study by headquarters estimated that the trucks with the soldiers would reach the area between the time of 16:15 hours and 16:40 hours on Monday 27th August 1979.

It was a Bank Holiday Monday and for the British it was to be the worst day that they had experienced since the start of the Troubles.

The fuses used had been utilized from a model aircraft remote control mechanism, and these were calibrated and the timings adjusted to activate the next day.

At 15:00 hours the two men who had unloaded the packages were slowly walking alongside the south bank of the Lough-both felt content, as all was well.

Also at 15:00 hours, eight soldiers were preparing themselves for the journey from the Ballykinier Barracks to the town of Newry and for six of them it would be their last.

The soldiers as expected were punctual, perfectly dressed and they assembled at the transport depot where they were inspected by the sergeant in charge.

He checked their itinerary and the load list, and dismissed the party with a salute.

The convoy consisted of one Land Rover and two four-ton lorries.

An hour before the soldiers left the barracks, the two casual looking men continued to stroll along the bank, each recapping on their instructions.

They had parked the car and were carefully selecting a place where they could see the convoy and activate the fuse.

At 16:36 hours the trucks came into view slowly moving along the road unaware of what lay ahead.

At precisely 16:40 hours the front lorry passed next to the truck with the milk pallets, and with that O'Donnell detonated the primary charge.

The whole area suddenly shook with intensity as half a ton of explosives blasted into the atmosphere.

With a tail of flame, the second truck lifted from the ground and seemed to be dumped on its side by an unforeseen hand.

Immediately after the blast there was silence, an eerie quiet followed by screams by both the two soldiers left alive and by onlookers realizing the horror.

The remains of the six dead soldiers were scattered across the road and into the bushes.

The blast was so fierce that the only thing remaining of the driver was his pelvis that was welded to the seat.

The marines in the first truck returned fire to the south side of the border.

Such was the response from the Royal Marines that within less than half an hour a Gazelle helicopter had dropped off the medical staff to support the eight men devastated in the first blast.

A second helicopter dropped off a new commanding officer and he immediately organized a fall-back situation.

Exactly thirty-two minutes after the first blast, another bomb was detonated – this time it was a huge 800 lb fertilizer device that rocked the area again, this time with even greater intensity.

The second blast was the worst category, with little left of the twelve soldiers killed under its savagery.

Body parts were strewn over the road and into trees and streams, with some vaporized by the heat.

A head was found in a stream, a face in the road and all that was left of the commanding officer was his epaulette.

In such circumstances it seems that the dead are dealt little respect, and the killers who planned such a cowardly act do not deserve respect now or in the future.

Even in war there are rules and human integrity is often forgotten in the heat of battle.

In the end it is left in the conscience of the predator; he will be alone when he meets his maker, and only on judgment day will he need to settle his account!

Pope John Paul sent a personal message to Queen Elizabeth. It mentioned both the Narrow Water Castle and the Sligo bombings that occurred the same day.

I offer to your Majesty my sincere condolences on the tragic murder of Lord Mountbatten, a courageous man whose death has caused grief to your family. This act of shocking violence is an insult to human dignity.

I condemn it, together with other acts of violence on the same day that caused death and brought suffering to many families. I ask Almighty God to be merciful to those who have died, to comfort their relatives, and to touch the hearts of the violent men with his healing grace.

7

Author's note:

Many Nationalists did not feel the same as this statement describes and felt that it was retribution for the Bloody Sunday massacre in 1972 when the British Army shot twenty-six civil rights' campaigners.

2

A RELIGIOUS THEME

The Irish in the South are predominantly a Catholic population administered by the Pope and his cardinals in the Vatican; the population in the North are predominantly Protestant, administered by the Church of England.

And what better reason to have a war than that between religions!

Both have the same God, the same book of righteousness and both religions are categorized as Christian.

It was events in history that changed the English national belief from Catholic to Protestant, brought about by a king of England.

Henry VIII, frustrated because of his differences with the Church over divorce, decided to break from Rome and instigate his own church.

This was to be administered by his own puppet clergy; only in this way could he control the right to divorce when and whom he wanted.

The king had grown tired of Catherine, his first wife, and at the time was lusting after a beautiful lady-in-waiting, Anne Boleyn.

Rome objected to his marriage to Catherine based on the fact that she was the widow of his brother.

He and his henchman, Cardinal Wolsey, were confident that their argument would persuade Rome to either grant a divorce or annul the marriage, and free Henry to marry Anne.

However, all this did little to change the Church, and the King, frustrated with the Vatican's bureaucracy, soon decided to take the situation in hand.

Henry introduced the mechanism that started the Reformation and included a clause in the new doctrine that granted the right of the monarch to divorce at his choice, and marry whoever.

But Henry during his reign made full use of his power, breaking from Rome and its Catholic rules, providing him with the supreme power he craved.

Many prominent people died as a result of the Reformation instigated by Henry, although the most glamorous must be his wife Anne Boleyn, the intelligent society lady who captured Henry VIII's heart, but was discarded by him after only three years of marriage.

Henry appears to have been captivated by Anne from the start and made positive moves to make her his mistress.

Henry soon realized that her response was not as positive as he wanted, and further to his investigations of her background he discovered that Anne was having an affair with another man, Henry Percy.

The King ordered Cardinal Wolsey to fix the situation, and "do whatever is necessary".

Wolsey worked the situation in his own underhanded way, and forced Percy to pull away from Anne and transfer his affections to another woman of Wolsey's choice, whom he promptly married.

After finding out that Wolsey was at the bottom of the split Anne vowed revenge on the Cardinal, and she may well have succeeded, as shortly after Cardinal Wolsey was executed for treason.

Anne did not fair too well either, and with the mysterious political situation prevailing with Henry at the time, she soon found herself in the Tower.

Henry trumped up many charges against his wife, and she was subsequently tried by jury and sentenced to death.

Among those on the jury who voted for the death penalty was her former lover, Henry Percy.

3

TWO FALLEN ANGELS

DECEMBER 1977

For two young men born and bred in Rostrevor, its beauty was of little solace, and they both hungered for more excitement; the patriotism that burnt inside them was the only path that they intended to tread, but the question that was on both their lips was "How?"

These two misguided young men went by the names of Barney Coughlin and Declan McBride.

Two young Catholic dissidents, they had over the passing years said farewell to many friends who left the village for pastures new, some going to England, others moving further afield to the United States and even as far as New Zealand.

The two of them had not been tempted to travel, even for a better life, because of the love and dependencies within their families.

Barney, with his ageing widowed mother and Declan, with his close association with a local girl by the name of Bridget McClory, had kept them on home soil.

They were young and both had developed work skills in the town, but life for them both had become a drag and they felt in a rut.

Barney was taken on as a young mechanic in the local garage, although from his appearance he looked more like a rough and tough farm boy from the country.

His hair fair bordering on red, with a broad forehead and open smiling face, he looked a bundle of mischief.

His pastimes were just as robust as he looked, entering all competitive events at the county fair although his speed on the running track did not impress.

Coming last was not an option for Barney and in his teens he joined a boxing club in the town of Warrenpoint and won six out of seven bouts as a welterweight. However, this was short-lived, as his work became more of a priority than his attendance at the boxing gym.

By the time he cleaned up after work there seemed nothing better to do than visit the pub.

As more of his friends left he became closer to Declan, and the two spent more time together, except when his friend was visiting his girlfriend Bridget.

Declan was also lucky with getting work and joined a local builder, first as a labourer then as he showed more aptitude he was taken on as an apprentice bricklayer where he learned everything from groundwork and foundations to plumbing and wiring.

The work hardened his slim frame and with his dark and brooding looks, he may have passed as a young Paul Newman.

But although these two boys were busy with work, others found it more difficult to find, including their friends who moved away looking for a better life.

The two young men stayed and continued their life in and around the town, but as the years rolled by, they felt life was going too fast and wanted more excitement.

Like all youths, they began to think that the world owed them something.

"Why are we the last of the boys from school to be left here, Declan?" Barney continued to complain, "Pat Lyden is a rich man in England, that dunce of a lad Eamon Fallon is a music teacher in Australia. How the fuck did we miss out?"

"It's not so bad, we at least have jobs, but life, I agree, is tedious at times." Declan was trying to cool the discussion.

"If it wasn't for my mam, I'm sure I would have been gone by now."

"I'm telling you it is the fucking British who have kept us down where they want us," Declan now agreed with Barney's bleating.

"All these years we have done what the politicians from London have wanted, and this half of Ireland is crap." Barney was now in full swing.

He went on, "I am telling yer that the British Government has treated the Irish people like domestic servants, like animal fodder, and we do nothing about it."

"Then we must do something rather than just talk," suggested Declan.

"I am with that, and want to be remembered as a true Irishman that did something for his country." Barney was now fantasizing. "You know, Barney, I dream that future generations will look at me in photos on the pub wall, and say 'What a man'."

"Now you are bloody dreaming," laughed Declan.

"No, I am telling yer, I will be, I know it!"

"And how?" Declan was probing.

"I'll tell yer how when it happens."

Declan's parents had moved south when his father retired and now lived in the west of Ireland. He had a cousin who lived nearby but did not see much of her. However, his association with Bridget was a most uncomfortable one. He had met her at school eight years earlier and the relationship seemed to be going nowhere.

They were originally attracted to each other through the Church, but his sexual intentions were quickly squashed at an early stage, when Bridget put her foot down firmly regarding any ideas that Declan might have about proving his manhood.

Both in their early twenties, they were constantly under media pressure, from the sex scenes that they watched on the television and at the movies.

Declan was a young man full of testosterone, his needs were paramount, they had to be fulfilled, but his young girlfriend was not responsive to his sexual aggression and the longer the relationship continued the more frustrated he became.

On one particular evening whilst both were watching a movie on television, there was a passionate scene that stirred them both; Bridget especially became aroused as the actors over emphasized their sexuality, the lighting and movement of the two naked bodies bringing out the most outrageous fantasy in her imagination.

She squirmed on the settee next to her partner restraining her urges for most of the film until she could not hold back any longer. He was taken completely by surprise when she launched herself upon him, kissing him with an open and very wet mouth, her hands grappling his face and chest. He responded slowly at first and after the initial surprise returned the passion. Grappling with her skirt, he slid his hand upwards on her leg, surprised when he felt that her stockings were held by a suspender belt.

"Not here, Declan. Let us move to my room in case Mother comes back," she said breathlessly.

Declan again was amazed that in such high feeling she could think of her mother coming back in a few minutes from a town thirty miles away.

"OK, let's go," he said, not giving it another thought.

Declan reached the bedroom, and he waited a few seconds for her before he switched off the light.

In an instant he reached for her, his hands fondling her body, they brushed down until with both his hands, he cupped them round her bottom.

He felt the elasticated top of her panties and the position of the line of the suspender belt support.

In such excitement and naivety he forgot to remove the clips from her stockings and belt, and by placing his hand on the inside of her panties pulled them down towards her ankles catching them on the suspender catch as he did so.

The more he pulled the more they got snagged.

"Stop, Declan, you are hurting me." She pushed him away and adjusted herself before switching on the light.

She pulled her skirt up to the waist and released the clips to her stockings, and immediately dropped her panties to the floor.

He moved forward again overcome with excitement with the sight of her standing nude from the waist down, her black stockings the only exception.

Moving expectantly towards her, he was again disappointed as she held him back with her straight arm; he was confused.

She, as always, was the power. Even now with passions high, she remained cold and calculating; he thought things would never change.

Bridget in control, stood legs apart; it was the last thing that Declan saw before she deftly switched out the light, then giggling rushed towards the bed and flopped backwards onto it.

Declan, still blinded by the sudden darkness, was guided by her laughter, and he made straight towards her, unbuttoning his trousers as he went; there was only one thing on his mind.

As he slid down onto her body he felt her complete nakedness, the excitement in him was unparalleled, it made him shake with excitement and he fumbled as he tried to find her, but without success, inexperience and excitement overcoming him.

Her breathing was now heavy and spasmodic, she was almost crying out in anticipation and eventually she placed her hand onto him, but gasped in amazement at his manhood.

She took control and it was her who finally guided him and they both started gyrating, soon both enjoying the new sensation, loudly making noises of appreciation, and passion.

In anticipation of the outcome they continued their new experience, and as if on cue, they simultaneously gasped loudly as they both fell together and lay motionless on the bed.

After only a few seconds, she pulled herself up and away, unfeeling and unceremoniously dumping him from the bed to the floor – he felt like fodder and rejected.

He looked up startled and drowsy, and could only focus on her naked body for a second as she ran from the bedroom shouting over her shoulder as she did so, "You did not take precautions, you are never ever considerate, especially now – you are an idiot."

After ten minutes she appeared at the bathroom door with a gown and a towel wrapped around her head.

She always felt she held control over Declan but this time it was different, she paused in the doorway, a look of surprise on her face, the room was empty, the door was ajar, the bird had flown.

4

POLITICS, A LOOSE WORD

The Irish Republican Army had been very active. Tensions ran high in Belfast and London, and it seemed there was no end in sight. Ordinary people without a political conviction quietly went their different ways, seeing no evil, speaking no evil and hearing no evil – breaking these rules could be the end for you and your family.

The divide was the Christian religion, the Protestants representing the UK and the Catholics representing 'all Ireland'.

The religious sects rarely mixed, and should they do so, it suggested to others it may be because of treachery or treason.

The ordinary people of Ireland wanted peace; the powerful and dangerous Provisional Republican Army wanted total freedom. It seemed to them that bombs and destruction might be the last and only resort.

The Troubles also brought opportunities even to those without a cause, the city street gangs prevailing, making the most of the divide.

The IRA needed a constant supply of weapons, and the procurement of these arms cost money.

It was necessary for them to have a source of reliable income, and this came from a variety of areas.

The United States had an immense Irish contingent and their fanatical supporters arranged fundraising gigs, pub collections and donations and the flow of money to support the arms requirement was adequately maintained.

Other more powerful sympathizers at home and abroad contributed by one means or another, either by money transactions or by arms.

The Soviet Union and Gaddafi's Libya, as always, were causing international mischief, and supplied arms, munitions and bomb-making material, right under the noses of the British.

The two young men from Rostrever both now at the ripe old age of twenty-three spent most of their spare time together, walking mile after mile, either talking about the latest village scandal or trying to put the world to right.

The subject always turned to 'the struggle' and what they both could do to help the situation and make a name for themselves.

Most of their conversations finished up in a whisper, as preventing loose talk was one of the golden rules that must be keep.

A SPLIT IN THE RANKS

In the first quarter of the twentieth century the situation became worse, with fighting between the Irish themselves.

In 1922 a treaty between the government of Lloyd George and the Chairman of the Provisional Irish Government, Michael Collins, was agreed and signed under controversial circumstances.

Although Collins was a powerful and respected man in Irish politics, he had moved without the overall consent of his government.

Collins was not a statesman, and had he adopted his position as envoy plenipotentiary he may have lost credence as a guerrilla leader, if hostilities resumed.

The reason that the Irish President de Valera did not head

up the delegation to England to negotiate the treaty was his own egoism.

De Valera had campaigned in the US, raising money for the cause under the title of President of the Republic, and when he found out the King of England would not be present at the treaty negotiations, he nominated a lower-ranked official, one Arthur Griffith, to lead the delegation and Collins to act as his deputy.

But Arthur Griffith suddenly fell ill, and it was left to Collins to negotiate a peace plan, between him and his London adversaries.

This occurred on 16th January 1922, but de Valera thought the terms were flawed, and felt as the President of the Republic that he had not had a say in the negotiations and in any case did not agree with the outcome.

There were many reasons why the people of Ireland did not want to go along with Griffith and Collins, and their anger would be vented accordingly.

It was claimed by Collins that as plenipotentiary on behalf of Ireland he had the power to do what he had to do, to resolve the situation.

He was a Crown-appointed Prime Minister, installed as such under a Royal Prerogative.

Politically both de Valera and Collins clashed head on, the former strongly opposed to the Anglo-Irish Treaty and in strong opposition to Collins.

On 14th April 1922, a group of anti-treaty IRA men demonstrated this by occupying the law courts in Dublin.

The British pressurized Collins to attack the men, and put a stop to this demonstration, which he did, reluctantly, bringing the men to trial and execution.

Although Collins was against the trial, he tried in vain to

rescue the men, and the resulting situation was the catalyst for civil war.

Collins knew of the potential consequences upon signing the treaty and actually predicted his own death.

During his stay in London whilst negotiating the agreement, Collins had resided at an address in west London.

Rumour was rife at the time that Collins had fallen in love with a British socialite who was a personal friend of Winston Churchill's. The situation developed even further when it was speculated that the British foreign secretary had instigated this liaison, manipulating the lady in question.

This claim was never proven but the action that Collins took was nevertheless a tragedy for Ireland, whether right or wrong, this decision split the country, and the outcome was inevitable.

This whole situation over the treaty created not only war but massive mistrust between the Irish people and the British Government and the differences would certainly be reflected in the in the Irish vote when it became appropriate.

Barney and Declan had grown up with the ideology of one Ireland governed by the Irish Government in Dublin.

Instead of peace, the bickering led to civil war, and the conflict with the British continued, the situation remaining tense.

The men who died for the cause were etched on Declan's and Barney's minds.

Those gallant Irishmen mentioned and recorded in past tales were hailed as heroes, and they wanted beyond anything else to follow in their footsteps.

Both swore that they would take the oath and join the Irish Republican Army, but where would they begin, and just how would they make contact with the army?

5

FANTASIES OF WAR

MARCH 1978

Early one Saturday morning in the spring of 1978 the two young men wandered up the narrow country lanes that zigzagged through the wet but beautiful mountainside.

It was here that the two could find the time and security to discuss the recent bombing that had occurred.

"Let's carve our name on the stone, Declan," suggested Barney enthusiastically.

"What, and join the enemy? Because nearly all the punters on the stone are from the UK," answered Declan.

"That's fantasy," said Barney, and added, "If we include our names on that stone we will be immortal, and if we scribe deep enough we will be remembered for centuries, with people reading out the name of Barney Coughlin, and Declan McBride."

"Remembered for what?" replied Declan. "I want to be remembered for something heroic, something that will make people say, 'what a hero'."

"You are fantasizing," laughed Barney, "and how may I ask will that happen?"

"I will tell you how," said Declan. "It will happen after we get sworn into the army and get asked to carry out an assignment that will shock the world." He paused. "That's how."

"I thought it would be better to rob a bank and die rich and in glory like *Butch Cassidy and the Sundance Kid*," laughed Barney.

"Be serious and bail out if you do not want the action, fair dos, but I am going to join the cause!" shouted Declan.

"And how will we do that, at the recruiting office?" said Barney.

"You are not being serious, and it is time for me to know if you are with me on this thing or not," said Declan in earnest.

"Sorry, my friend, for the sarcasm, but I am with you totally, wholeheartedly. But I ask myself... How?"

Declan answered, "I will show you." They both walked together slowly, shoulders together, along the downhill path to the village pub.

The next day the boys met and again walked the hilly roads, when Declan broke the silence and said, "Tomorrow we join. Are you ready?"

"Our situation is getting confusing, Declan. How the bloody hell are we going to do that? Walk into the recruiting office and say, here we are?"

"Yes," said Declan. "Almost, but the recruiting office is the local pub, and we just drop a hint to the landlord."

"And how do we do that?" said Barney. "Just tell the landlord that we are going to blow up the Houses of Parliament?"

"Barney, you are too fucking negative, and we will see what you are made of when we are in." With that Declan stalked off into the night, disgusted that his best mate did not have the same passion as himself.

A few days passed and the boys had not met, so Barney phoned his friend. "Sorry about the other night. Let's have a chat at the pub later."

"I'm going to give it a miss, Barney. Sorry but I feel rotten, really ill, the flu has me bad. Let's make it next week when I am feeling better."

"Sure." Barney put the phone on the hook, walked sternly out of the house and made for the pub, with one thing on his mind.

He was hurting regarding the impression that Declan had of him, suggesting that his heart was not in 'it'. "I will make him eat those words!" Barney was mad.

It was near opening time and the pub lounge was quiet, but in an hour it would be busy with the workers arriving for a drink on their way home.

Barney bought his pint from Kelly the barmaid, and the two of them were the only people in the bar at the time.

After serving him his pint, she walked away from the bar and Barney seized his chance.

"Miss Kelly, would you know how the fuck we join the army?"

"The army?" replied Kelly. "And who is we, and why do you want to get involved in that shit?" She pursed her lips.

"It's just that Declan and I are sold on the thing and helping the cause whatever way we can," answered Barney.

"To be sure, that is dangerous talk in a pub," said Kelly sternly. "I do not want to hear anything more of that nonsense from your mouth, as this type of talk will get us both killed."

Barney felt he had betrayed himself by talking to Kelly so freely, and was now worried whether she would mention the conversation to the local police.

He sipped his pint, then waited until Kelly moved from the bar area and he silently slipped out of the door and into the cold night air.

6

A MOVE NORTH

FEBRUARY 1978

Martin Valeron was changing jobs, and had decided that his future lay in North Sea oil. He worked for a large company that was associated with the oil and gas industry.

The development of North Sea oil was still in its infancy and his work at the moment was either feast or famine, resulting in inconsistent labour demands; in other words, unreliable.

One minute the recruitment agencies were head-hunting everyone they could lay their hands on, and at other times, the demand for people was uneventful.

The company where he worked could not secure an order book that could sustain the present workforce and it was becoming obvious that redundancies were inevitable.

To survive he needed to 'bite the bullet' and change direction, even if it meant moving from a comfy seat in the office to a cold and draughty construction site.

Construction work paid well and the time spent on site normally exceeded the time spent on design and engineering in the office, and with the extra hours he thought that this was the way to go.

He applied for work at a number of main contracting companies and chose the most appealing: one that paid the most money. This happened to be the biggest construction site in the world at the time.

The offer was made and he accepted it wholeheartedly; he now looked forward to working at Sullom Voe, the oil terminal currently under construction.

The accommodation for workers in the Shetland Islands was limited. It was the oil company's strategy to do as much work on the mainland as possible, liquidating many hours, before transporting the structures to site with minimal hours left to be done. This method of construction was known as modularization.

Sullom Voe (the Voe) was on the northern area of Shetland, its location about an hour's drive along narrow and slow roads to the main town of Lerwick.

Before hydrocarbons were discovered, the islanders experienced only fishing as a main industry; with the fattest seagulls in the world, it was a wonder that they ever got airborne.

There are not many places in the world with such hostile living conditions, the weather so depressing, rain expected almost on a daily basis, the wind sometimes reaching over a hundred kilometres an hour.

During the winter months, daylight is reduced to almost five hours, and if that is not bad enough, the sky is almost never without cloud coverage.

The new process plant on the terminal was to be the largest of its kind in the world and also the biggest section of the terminal.

The cost of the process area represented nearly 40% of the total cost of the terminal. It was designed to handle nearly 1.5 million barrels of crude oil a day.

The main pipeline stretching from the offshore wells to the terminal covered over one hundred miles with plans already underway for an extension of the line.

Martin left the offices of his current employers in Barrow, Cumbria, and headed south for his new work in west London.

He had decided on the change after two years with the company, mainly due to the threat of redundancy, and thought that London was more of a hub than Barrow.

As he left the offices, the receptionist called after him.

He was in a hurry to catch the train, the interception from her was annoying but in a polite gesture he turned and smiled to find out what she wanted.

"Martin, a call came through for you earlier, and he has since rung again at least twice."

"Who was it? The taxman?" enquired Martin.

"He seemed intense, and said to call him as soon as you could."

"Who was it?" said Martin

She looked down at her notes.

"He said his name was George Webster, and said you would know his number."

"Yes I do, that's fine, I will call him later, and good luck in the future. I must be off to catch the train."

After arriving in London he was told to head out to the construction offices in Hertfordshire where he was briefed before heading north.

He had not forgotten his promise to the receptionist to call George, whom he had not spoken with for some time.

The train journey from Kings Cross to Glasgow was uneventful and his time was spent reading the newspapers with the occasional nap promoted by the rhythmic sound of wheels over rails.

He started on the sports page at the back of the paper and worked his way to the front, and it was only when he reached the final page did he realize the horrors that had occurred the night before.

The headlines spread over the front page could have been printed in blood.

12 KILLED IN THE LA MON RESTAURANT IN NORTHERN IRELAND

The restaurant is located twelve miles from Belfast and a petrol bomb exploded at 21:00 hours on 17th February.
It was of the type used in Vietnam with napalm mixed with petrol.
This was to maximize distress in the victims because of the adhesive nature of the mixture.
A warning came only nine minutes before the blast, and the IRA claimed responsibility.
It was probably the distasteful and most uncivilized action so far in the Irish Troubles.
Two children also died in the explosion.

Martin was stunned, his mouth dry and eyes wet from tears thinking of the children burnt alive, and he prayed that they died without pain.

He left the train at New Street station in Glasgow on the morning of 18th February, and headed for the station's taxi rank.

How far, he thought, *would the Irish nationalists go in their attempt to draw attention to their goals?*

He was away with his own thoughts when suddenly the Glaswegian taxi driver shouted, "Glasgow airport!"

His flight from Glasgow to Sumburgh in Shetland was

due to depart at 10:00 hours and this gave him time for some refreshment.

He looked for the 'check-in' desk of Dan-Air, the chartered carrier that operated to Shetland.

In its bid to win the contract with the oil company, Dan-Air had purchased seven Hawker Siddeley 748 – series 1 aircraft from Argentina – and it was these that were to ferry oil workers over the next four years.

The aircraft was a twin turbo prop and could carry up to forty-four passengers.

They were later nicknamed 'budgies' by the people who flew in them. These aircraft were used continually on a daily basis shuttling workers backwards and forwards to their work.

At the peak of the work, up to five thousand contractors were ferried between the mainland and the Shetland Islands.

Flights were available from most airports in the UK but those most associated with the oil workers were from Glasgow, Belfast and Newcastle.

It was in these places where the skills required at Sullom Voe were originally obtained, but with the shipyards closed, the skills of the redundant men were available if they were willing to travel.

Apart from the Dan-Air charter flights, Sumburgh also provided a scheduled service to the mainland.

The duration of the working day changed in the oil industry dramatically from the workers grafting for twelve hours a day, seven days a week to a more sedate eight hours a day for five days a week.

The men's prosperity suffered and the unions and health and safety regulators were not popular, but it was sensible and necessary.

The oil operators knew that any fatalities caused by unsafe working could set back the industry, and cost them dearly in the long run, so they agreed wholeheartedly to the changes.

The work pattern at Sullom Voe was set by the oil company and consisted of three weeks working at twelve hours a day and a week at home for rest and recovery.

The offshore working rota was also revised and most companies worked two weeks offshore and two weeks at home.

7

SCUD MISSILE

FIVE YEARS EARLIER

The first time that Martin heard of the Scud missile was in Egypt in 1973 during a cessation of hostilities during the Yom Kippur war between Israel and Egypt.

Instigated by Anwar el-Sadat the war started on 6th October 1973; this date is most significant to the Israelis, as it is Yom Kippur – the Jews' most celebrated holiday.

The war lasted only five days. It started when the Egyptians together with Syria and Jordan attacked Israel, and the intention was to recover an area of land lost to Israel six years earlier.

Initially the attack took the Israelis by surprise, but they retaliated quickly and effectively, overcoming the opposition in this short time.

After purchasing Scud missiles from North Korea, Egypt had the intention to use these in the war but did not have the opportunity over this short period.

Just previous to the attack Egypt and the Russians had surveyed one potential area near to Port Said that was to be a potential launching site.

However, the Israelis' intelligence was sufficiently astute to counter this plan and in an attempt to delay the Egyptian offensive fired their missiles, destroying the area under preparation.

After the ceasefire Egypt wanted to recover its status quickly, with Port Said the main priority; Egypt was still intent on using the area.

To expedite the situation, they used foreign contractors to renovate the war damage, with the intention to regroup their armed forces as soon as possible.

When Martin arrived as part of the clean-up operation, he was amazed at the carnage that the Israelis' attack had caused, with twisted steel, still smouldering buildings and the acrid smell of expended munitions still in the air.

He had never experienced the devastation of war, and was shocked at the outcome.

The first day he worked hard, but at nightfall, exhausted and dirty, he desperately wanted a shower, food and sleep.

His first task was to find his accommodation block, one of many surrounding the site.

He had the key, block and room number but the room numbers were not in chronological order and with the language difficulties it was harder than he'd first thought.

His perseverance paid off and he soon found himself standing outside what looked more like a Wild West army fort than an accommodation block.

Inside the stockade it was more organized, with no damage from the attack, it had neat pathways and some colourful plant life, but the accommodation building was hideous, a huge steel canister painted grey with slit-type windows; it looked like a jail, and he hoped it was better inside than it appeared outside.

He was fortunate to be allocated a single room. Although it was tiny it included a bed and a shower but little else.

However, if he could sleep later, it would be a luxury and he wanted for nothing but first a shower, then to the mess for food; he needed to be quick before the hungry masses descended.

He was lucky: the mess was almost empty when he arrived, so he grabbed a meal and a tray at the hatch and sat at the first table that he found.

Soon others joined him and with the table full, Martin scanned those sharing his table.

On his left were two very smart Egyptian army officers who conferred with each other quietly, and on his left two Russians, the larger of the two already stuffing bread into his mouth.

He was a big man, wearing a scruffy beard and unkempt hair, his clothes those he had worn all day; they were soiled from site work.

Loud and cheerful, he was, it seemed, much different to his companion, who was slim, short, his face shaven.

At the top of the table directly opposite Martin sat a small shifty looking North Korean.

It seemed a surreal situation and not knowing whether they spoke English or not, he opened the conversation.

"Hi guys, my name is Martin Valeron, and I am manager of the offsite renovation area."

There was no counter introduction that followed other than the big Russian who smiled and nodded silently.

Martin continued and ignoring the lack of retort, spoke out, "I am British and this is my first day. Can I ask, if it is not classified information, what you guys are up to?"

One of the Egyptians spoke up, "Argh, British, that's good."

By the interest shown, it seemed that the North Korean and the smaller of the two Russians could not speak English.

The soldier continued, "Mr Martin, we are part of a team working on Scud missiles recently purchased by the Egyptian Government from the North Koreans. It is interesting to note, sir, that since the purchase we have not fired a missile in anger, yet we have a large team mobilized here."

"Scud missiles; sorry but I know little about arms, I am a construction engineer," advised Martin as he interrupted the soldier.

"That is fine, Mr Martin, but you will understand that I cannot speak in specifics concerning my work, but I can tell you basically what a Scud is."

The soldier paused and looked down at the table and collected his thoughts.

"The original Scud was a surface to surface missile and designed by the Nazi scientist Werner Von Braun, and for all intents and purposes it is the same today although perhaps a modernized version, you understand. Since the Second World War and as a guest of the Russians he developed it further."

The large Russian smiled and nodded in understanding.

"You will appreciate that the first design was called initially the V2 and used against your country."

He continued, still looking at the table. "The Soviets developed it further and it was called R11, R17 and so on. Now the North Koreans are in the act and have developed their own version as Mr Lee would tell you if he could speak in English to you. You see, Mr Martin, the Scud is a derivative designed and changed by the designer, but in general terms the range is approximately two hundred miles."

In a heavy accent the Russian spoke, "The range will depend on the type of Scud and the weight of the warhead." He smiled, and was pleased to add to the conversation.

The second Russian stood up and headed for the bar, but was back in a few moments with four vodkas and two juices.

He held up his hand to wait as he trudged back to the bar to bring a further four vodkas.

Sitting down he passed the juices to the two Egyptians and the vodka he split evenly with the others at the table.

The larger Russian watched and when his friend was ready picked up one of the drinks and held it in the air.

"We drink now for peace and love." In a loud voice he cried out: "Nostrovia!" and sank the two drinks.

Over the next four days that Martin was on site, the dinner in the evening followed the same pattern although each time the number of vodkas increased.

His work was completed by the fifth day and he departed by taxi, and headed for Cairo.

He had enjoyed the company at the table in the mess and had learnt something in the bargain.

A CHANCE MEETING

In Cairo, the airport was closed but due to a ceasefire it was expected to open during the next few days.

Martin thought that things would not happen that quickly and decided to check in at the Marriott on the Nile, close to downtown Cairo, and made his way to the hotel.

The weather was warm, the swimming pool ice blue, the parasols fluttered in the mild breeze, and he could not wait to enjoy the time at the Marriott, doing nothing more than relaxing.

It seemed a good place to be, providing the war did not resume, and he would make the most of it.

He arrived at the hotel and joined the queue waiting to check in. Standing about sixth in line, he made conversation with the man standing behind.

He looked the businessman type: blue suit, white shirt and he carried a small leather handbag and a small suitcase.

"Travelling makes me feel tired and uncouth, and there you are, sir, looking fresh as a daisy; have you travelled far?"

The man was relaxed and seemed to take the question in his stride. He laughed but gave Martin a gaze that was like steel, as if assessing him.

A thought crossed Martin's mind that the guy did not speak English. "Thank you, but I have just arrived by road after sitting for eight hours, so I do not feel as fresh as you kindly say. I cannot wait to get in the shower, and wash this sand from my hair."

The queue moved up a couple of notches and Martin continued the conversation. "Today I have arrived from Port Said carrying out some work repairing the war damage, but glad to be on my way back to the UK, that's if anything flies out of here."

"That's interesting; you know this business is not over yet, so you may be back." The man seemed confident with his remarks.

Martin moved towards the desk to check in and turned to say goodbye, but as he did so the man said, "If you are free later, please join me for dinner. I will not be staying up long as I have a long flight in the morning."

"That seems great; what about seven, or seven thirty?" suggested Martin.

"Fine; see you in the restaurant then."

Martin was at the table first, and opened the *The Economist* to catch up with the latest political situation around the Middle East, but it was only a minute or so before his friend from 'check in' joined him so he put his magazine down.

"By the way, my name is George, eh, George Webster," he said, extending his hand.

"Martin Valeron." They shook hands and both sat down.

"Eh, did you tell me what did the damage?" enquired George.

"No I did not, but it may have been a Scud missile, at least a missile of sorts." Martin smiled.

The waiter arrived and both decided on a main course, the rib-eyed steak.

George ordered a bottle of wine at an exorbitant price, and followed up with a nod to Martin.

"Don't worry, old chap, this is going on expenses, my treat." He smiled.

They both fell silent for a few minutes, and waited for the waiter to pour George a little wine for tasting.

The waiter then poured the two glasses and left the table and the men to continue their conversation.

"Those things, the Scuds I mean, do not seem to have changed since the Blitz." George seemed eager to pursue the conversation about the Scud.

The knowledge that Martin had learnt from the Egyptian officer started to flow.

"Von Braun, the Nazi arms engineer, really started something; the size now is the same as when he designed the original."

"Yes, that's right, it is still 0.88m," answered George who seemed to know his stuff.

"It is the storable propellant that is the advantage over other types of missiles and can be prepared for launching quickly." Martin was in full swing.

He continued to share his knowledge about Scuds, and the conversation continued throughout the meal.

Immediately after they had finished, the waiter collected the plates and brought the bill to George who signed it.

"What do you do?" asked Martin.

"Oh, I work for the Home Office, you know, a diplomat." George seemed tentative. "Here is my card." Martin noticed the cabinet emblem at the top. "I must go, my friend, I have an early rise in the morning, but perhaps I can take your number, and we can catch up when you are in London next. Please give me a ring when you can, we can catch up over a drink or a meal."

He smiled, shook hands with Martin and headed towards the lift.

8

MOBILIZATION 1

FEBRUARY 1978

Martin's flight took him from Glasgow to Sumburgh airport on the south tip of the Shetland Islands, then he travelled two hours by bus from the airport to the accommodation.

There was also another airport, called Scatsca, formerly used by the RAF, that was much closer to the terminal. Old and unsuitable it was being modernized, and was expected to be completed in about two months.

Travelling from Shetland in 1978 was restricted to flights from Sumburgh or ferries from Lerwick.

When Martin arrived at Sullom Voe he was in awe of the magnitude of the operation, especially with the logistics involved with flights, buses and the accommodation camps.

He made note that the main gate to the Toft camp was at the bottom of the hill with the whole accommodation built high overlooking the water.

The bus from the airport was scheduled to stop at pre-allocated points with the Mossbank bungalows first, then the hotel and lastly the two accommodation camps called Firth and Toft.

Looking out from the camp over the water one could see the island of Ulsta; a ferry from there was just arriving at Toft.

It rained heavily the day Martin arrived, it was almost

continuous and the streams of water rushed down the hill and gushed over his shoes as he stepped towards the cover of the reception.

For a moment he stopped, the rain still running down his face, and he took stock of his whereabouts, the men, the buildings and what looked like a city of wooden huts on the hill.

This was to be his home over the next few years.

The accommodation was tidy and the rows of huts seemed to go on forever up Toft Hill.

To his left was the road that he had just come into the camp on and beyond that was a coastal bay-type of area called the Voe and as far as the eye could see were the mysteries of the Shetland Islands.

He entered the building, handed over his passport, company details and position and waited for the administration clerk to find his details and guide him on his way.

The clerk looked up and took stock of the face in front of him.

"We normally like to accommodate the more senior staff further up the hill in more premium rooms, but for the time being you will need to make do because we are short of housing." With that he handed Martin his pack of information.

As the clerk moved on to deal with the next person in the line, he quickly turned and as an afterthought said to Martin, "You will need to pay a monthly subscription to the social club, which actually runs all the facilities here at Toft and at the other camp, Firth. You are bound by their rules and I included a copy of them in your welcome pack. Also included is a map of both camps and the facilities offered to you."

He went on, reciting every word the same way as he had done so many hundreds of times before. "There are three social centres at Toft each with bar, gymnasium and shop. Apart from the main areas, there are small conference facilities that include recreational rooms and vending machines."

He paused, then added, "There is absolutely no sympathy for extreme drunkenness or mixing of the sexes in the accommodation, and if this occurs the offender will have his social card taken from him and he will be banned from the camps and sent home and if this occurs – the action is non-negotiable."

The clerk turned back to the next man, who was incredibly patient and still had his arm held high waiting for the clerk to take his credentials.

Martin went to his room and found it comfortable but small.

Although the room contained a bed, desk, wardrobe and television set, by seven o'clock he was bored and decided to explore the area outside.

His accommodation was well up the hill so he ambled down towards the social area named on the map as the 'Northern Centre'.

On the way down he met a couple of elderly workers walking up the hill and asked the way.

"Say, can you guys point me towards the Wellie bar, or is it the Northern Centre?"

"Yoos just arrived?" said the taller of the two.

"Yes."

"Then you doona wanna go to the Wellie bar, laddie."

"Why not? On the introduction pack it describes it as the biggest centre and the best for a drink," said Martin.

"And the worst, especially wid yoos southern accent," added the tall man. He added as a matter of fact, "It's doon the hill on the right, yoos canna miss it," and he laughed and turned to carry on.

"Well, thank you, but I can look after myself." Martin shrugged.

"Yoos need to, mate, but good luck anyway." With that the men continued to walk slowly up the hill.

Martin made his way down, and reached a tall wooden building. Pulling back the double doors he walked in to the hallway. Ahead of him were two more doors, the one on the right was labelled Gym and the other to the left, Bar.

There was a hum of noise coming from the left-hand door and he slowly approached and opened it, then a cacophony of sound hit him; the noise sounded like a football stadium on a Saturday afternoon.

In front of him was what could be best described as a wild and rowdy establishment.

The room was long, spanning about 30 metres, with a bar running down the left-hand side almost the whole length of the building. Apart from various bodies leaning against the bar, the rest of the room had lines of tables filled with both women and men. It was difficult to tell the difference between the sexes because the majority wore fur-tipped parkas.

The noise continued, punctuated with screams, clinking of glasses and the drone of heavy conversation. The large barmaid had her elbows on the bar and was shouting in a coarse southern English tongue at a man who had collapsed onto his drink at the bar in front of her.

"If you cannot behave your fucking selves then get the fuck out of this bar."

She changed tack and suddenly started at other offenders and this time was addressing two burly men who had gripped each other's lapels.

"I'll knock his fucking head off!" shouted the ginger-bearded man in a gruff Scottish accent.

"You'll knock nobody's head off while I'm here, so sit down and pack it in or get the fuck out of here."

"You know the rules, Alistair, fight and you will be on your bike," added the burly barmaid.

Martin studied her and noticed that she was no beauty, and

no spring chicken. He estimated that she was between fifty and sixty, with a huge cleavage pulled up by a tight bra and blouse. She had small dark eyes and a huge hooked nose, and without a tooth in her head, looked even more grotesque when she shouted!

She continued glaring at the two offenders but did not look any less fearsome with her mouth closed.

The two burly men sought some refuge from the situation and sat on chairs about 10 metres from each other but continued to outstare each other.

Martin then noticed that there were also two men and two younger girls who stood looking at the older woman, and they all looked scared out of their wits in fear of the older woman at the bar.

One of the young girls was aged about twenty years old, and she joined the four waiting to be served. She was a young wisp of a girl who appeared more aggressive than the others but seemed a little unsteady on her feet. Her hair was blonde, possibly from a bottle, and was slightly dishevelled, but she had a small elfish but pretty face. He could not make out any other features of her body because it was draped in a blue parka. She reached the bar almost fatuously because her legs did not seem part of her body.

"Vee, give me four quadruple whiskies and two triple double gin and tonics.

"Lulu babe, are you sure you can make this, because tomorrow is Monday and there's a long week ahead of you," asked Vee.

"Vee, just pour the fucking drinks, and then we are going home," answered the girl.

Another of the girls staggered up to the bar and helped Lulu back to the table.

"And, young man, what would you like to drink this fine

night? From the look of you, this will be your first night I venture, especially with clothes like that on," she mocked him.

"A pint please," Martin asked Vee as nicely as possible.

"My name is Vee, actually it is short for Violet, and I run this bar," said the huge barmaid. "And with an accent like that you best keep yourself to yourself," she said as she pulled the pint.

Suddenly from the other end of the bar there was a disturbance.

"No I donna wanna come to your fucking house tonight," said the girl. "I'm tired and need my sleep, so piss off and I'll see you in ten years' time," shouted the girl.

"Don't be so fucking smart with all these people about; let's pack up and go," soothed the man.

Vee snapped to the young barmaid next to her. "Finish this pint, Mary, and I will get this little fucker off to his bed pronto."

A little time later and the man had disappeared, the female staying behind for a nightcap, by now with two other male friends who were buying the drinks.

Martin had seen enough and slowly moved to the doors and to the outside world.

It was quiet and very cold and the rain had frozen into small snowflakes, but the cold wind made the night feel miserable, and he started up the hill towards his accommodation.

Only a few yards later, he stopped in his tracks because right in front of him lay the body of a man, curled up in the recovery position and wearing the stock-in-trade parka jacket.

Martin stooped down to see if the man was conscious but in the second before he could reach him, he felt a strong hand on his shoulder pulling him back.

He slowly turned round to see a huge bearded male standing behind him, and he growled with a strong Glasgow accent, "Wait a second, yee ne'ir can be too careful, so stand aside and let me take a look see."

44

This huge giant of a man grabbed the man's left arm as if to pin the inert figure to the ground, then slowly turned him sideways, and then said to Martin without looking up, "You must be careful in case the man is armed, but this guy is not, and so pissed he is a danger to himself, and not to others. If I turn him he may vomit and choke, so find his key in his pocket and we will carry him home on my back, but as I say, keep your distance in case he throws up."

Martin guided the Good Samaritan with the drunk on his back to the address on the key tag, and they gently rested him on the bed, took his shoes off and quietly left the room.

"You know, laddie, that aboot a dozen souls have been found in this camp dead in their beds, drowned in their own vomit."

"That's amazing," stammered Martin. The large man threw a wave and disappeared into the night, and that was the last time that Martin ever saw him.

9

AN ENGLISHMAN
AT THE TERMINAL

FEBRUARY 1978

The next day Martin caught the site bus that took him the twenty minutes from the accommodation block to the site.

The bus was packed tight with oil workers and not a word was said. Each of the men was dressed the same with the standard issue parkas and loose-fitting boots called jalopies.

The bus stopped at the terminal gate where everyone disembarked and walked through security to the other side where another bus was waiting to shuttle the men to their workplace.

Martin's office was temporary at least until the more established building was finished on top of the hill. This office was positioned in the middle of the process area and the building was long and narrow with space for two offices abreast of each other and the corridor down the centre.

He was met by the office manager and shown to his own office. It was close to the door opening to the site but he did not mind and noted the label on the door, 'Design Office'.

The DCC carried out the design of the terminal and followed up, managing the site on behalf of the oil company also called the operator. The main construction contractor was a Glasgow company, and it controlled all the black trades on the site. Black trades were predominantly work associated with structural, fitting, and welding. The main construction contractor let out work to smaller companies, these naturally called sub-contractors.

Hours worked during a day were closely monitored for efficiency and safety and any lost hours due to accidents were called 'lost time indices'.

It occurred to Martin after the first few visits that a three-week stay on the island seemed longer each time he did it, and he needed a pastime outside of work, and that did not mean more frequent visits to the Wellie bar.

SOCIALIZING IN THE GYMNASIUM – MARCH 1978

After each day on site Martin returned to his accommodation tired in mind and weary of body. He needed some physical gym work to keep his body in condition and decided to make the effort and get down to the gym a few days a week.

One evening he packed his old skipping rope, tracksuit bottoms, white T-shirt and running shoes into a holdall and made for the Northern Centre gymnasium.

A PT instructor met him at the door and introduced himself as Barry White. The instructor explained that an exercise class would take place at the Northern Centre every night starting at eight o'clock.

He informed him that, "Its users are free to do what they like, but are welcome to join the camp fitness programme if they want." He added as a second thought, "It's me who runs the fitness programme." Barry explained that he worked on a rota with three other qualified gym instructors.

Martin took his time at the gymnasium office and decided to try and extract as much local knowledge from the PT instructor as he could. He was helpful and receptive, willing to answer any questions Martin posed, in his dry Geordie way.

The two talked for some time, and the instructor familiarized Martin with the gym and the people who used it.

Barry explained his own situation. "I work on a contract basis with a services company. It acts as my agent as it were for the work that I do here in the gym."

He went on, "My main occupation before I arrived here was as a professional boxer, back in Newcastle that is."

Barry paused, thinking of what he needed to add. "My duties here pay well and my intention was to resume the boxing after here, but my time might have expired by then. The truth is, Martin, that I can earn far more money here on a regular basis than I could in fighting for a living back home, and that is the bottom line." He shrugged to emphasize it was a no-brainer.

His very broad accent was difficult to understand, especially for Martin born and bred near to London. He changed in the dressing room and headed for the large hall; inside he saw there were about forty or so men doing various exercises. Most seemed overweight, and wandered about listlessly, and it was obvious to Martin that most of the men needed some sort of organizing and gym preparation before they actually started their exercise.

A group of guys were playing basketball at the top end of the hall whilst at the other end others were kicking a ball at the small goals normally used for five-a-side football. In the middle of the hall a small group of men were watching two boxers sparring with each other.

Martin thought it looked like murder rather than boxing as one guy, his shorts covered in ABA badges, was beating the other mercilessly, punch after punch, with the guy covered in blood. The three or four guys watching showed no emotion and did little to stop the onslaught.

There were no ropes that depicted the fight area, and the poor recipient did little to 'go on a run' away from his aggressive opponent.

In one corner of the gym, and completely isolated, another man was skipping with beads of sweat running down his face. His aide was closely looking at his stopwatch and suddenly came to life shouting, "Time!"

"How'er yer going, young fella," said the man holding the rope, and he grabbed the towel from his assistant and mopped his forehead.

"Fine," said Martin. "I have just got here and came in for a spot of training."

"Have yer dun a bit?" said the man in a strong Northern Irish accent.

Martin nodded. At this stage he really did not want to get involved.

"My name is Johnnie Caldwell," said the man, "and I hope that you enjoy your stay."

"Thank you," said Martin. "But if I remember rightly, you were a professional boxer, so I am surprised you are not with the group over there." He pointed to the group in the middle of the hall.

"I am too old to mix with these youngsters and besides, I like to train by myself; as you say, I was a professional, and those guys are a bunch of amateurs."

Martin looked at the man in front of him, and tried to visualize the likeness of the person that he remembered watching on the black and white television many years before.

Johnnie Caldwell was a bantamweight and a ruthless puncher in his weight division and won the world bantamweight championship.

At the time when he was world champion it meant that

he was a *true* world champ, not one of many for each weight division.

Martin recalled, thinking back over the years, when Caldwell lost his championship in ten rounds of a scheduled fifteen rounds to a Brazilian boxer by the name of Eder Jofre.

Jofre was a tremendous puncher who was later voted by *Ring* magazine to be in the top ten boxers of all time. So the man standing in front of him now was special in terms of famous boxers.

Caldwell was obviously not the man he once was, his face red and blotchy from drink, and his eyes narrow and bloodshot, but he still handled the skipping rope skilfully, probably from the thousands of times that he'd gone through the routine.

Johnnie Caldwell was from Northern Ireland and was a super bantamweight fighter who won the Golden Gloves in America as an amateur and later the world title as a professional.

Some months later when Martin got to know Caldwell better, he told him that the fight arrangements for his world title fight with Jofre were a farce, and alleged that Jack Solomon, his manager/promoter, hadn't even provided a contract for the fight.

Martin also discovered that two days before the fight he was taken to a professional football match and halfway through the match the referee made some critical mistakes in a match that meant the home team lost. It was to be the referee's last mistake as he was shot dead on the field right in front of him.

As Martin walked to the end of the large hall he noticed a net curtain and thought it would be a good place to hide and carry out his exercises in relative privacy. Caldwell walked half-way with him, and whispered in Martin's ear, "We will have a drink in the bar one night, young 'un, and I will explain to you the people who you shouldn't mix with."

"Who do you mean?" asked Martin.

"The Ulstermen, of course." And with that he clapped a hand on his back and walked away.

Martin climbed behind the curtain and removed his gear and started skipping, and as the rhythm picked up so did the beads of sweat on his brow. It was a few minutes later that one of the guys who had been watching the two boxers sparring in the middle of the gym came across and motioned Martin to stop and have a chat.

"You have done a bit of boxing looking at the way yer doing yer skipping," said the tousle-haired man.

The man held out his hand to introduce himself. "My name is Robby Burns, and I am here in Shetland for my sins, and working as a pipe fitter on the site at the same place as wee John whom I noticed yer were talking to," said the man.

"Yes, I did a bit as an amateur up to county championship class," answered Martin.

"Won't you join us?" invited Robby and slowly walked away with Martin in tow.

The two men sparring had stopped and the one doing all the attacking and punching was introduced to Martin as Ronny Relton, and as he did so Martin noticed all the ABA badges on his blue shorts.

The other man sparring was Nigel White the brother of the PT instructor at the reception. The two other guys watching were also boxers but had not decided at this time to put the gloves on.

As White stopped, the attention turned to Martin and he invited him to put the gloves on with Relton.

As they matched up for the first round of three, Martin had no intention of matching blow for blow and used his feet to move away from harm's way.

Relton persisted and his aggression was threatening. Martin brought his jab into play and using his right cross, he was only lucky once to catch his opponent solidly low on the face. This move brought some respect from Relton and the remaining session went without much ado.

Martin must have done okay, because when Robby removed the heavy sixteen-ounce gloves from him he said, "Yoos did well; in fact, you were the master." His lilting Edinburgh accent sounded almost poetic.

As they rubbed themselves down, Martin asked the guys if there was a boxing club at the camp or just an excuse to come to the gym.

"Naw, I am a professional fighter from Manchester," said the smaller of the guys, "but I get more money here on the terminal than in the ring, so the missus gives me no option, and I work here."

"Would you box here if there was a promotion?" asked Martin.

They all nodded. "Aye, we certainly would. If the missus permits it."

10

AN OPENING ARRIVES

The two young men were back to their routines, and after Barney told Declan about the episode with Kelly, both had gone about their business sheepishly, because they knew if Kelly had mentioned this to any of her customers then they could be made laughing stocks, and they could hear the taunts from the bar in their minds. Both avoided the pub for some time, and only went in for a pint when they found out that Kelly was not on duty.

Late in the month, Barney left the garage early and tried to look normal as he strode from work still wearing his overalls. He was excited and could not wait to find his mate, who was working on a house somewhere on the road towards Warrenpoint.

Barney knew it was close to the roadside because Declan had complained to him about the noise of the traffic. He drove slowly and covered the twelve miles or so in twenty minutes but he tried to keep calm. He had some news for his friend.

Suddenly he saw a house with scaffolding down one side. A few vehicles were parked near the roadside. *It must be where he is working*, Barney thought.

"Is Declan about?" he shouted to a painter on the top scaffold.

"To be sure, he was," shouted the man. "But I think he has

left early, and has gone home. Perhaps in the pub," shouted the painter.

Fuck my luck, thought Barney, annoyed that Declan hadn't let him know.

Driving back, he cursed the time he'd had off and the wasted petrol money. Then he saw Declan's car by the roadside and pulled alongside.

"Why the fuck don't you let me know when you leave work?" He did not wait for an answer. "I tell yer, Declan, I have had a word and I think we have the call," whispered Barney.

"What are you talking about?" Declan asked

"I was asked to look at a car that had broken down up by the McMahons' farm," added Barney excitedly.

"So what?"

"To be sure when I got there it was nothing but a loose electrical lead."

"And?"

"The guy asked if the pub was a good one and if I knew a barmaid called Kelly."

"Go on."

"I told him that I did. He asked what my friend's name was. To be sure, I said, it is Declan. He then asked me if we were in a position to do some work for him, and when I agreed, he asked if we could meet him there, the same place, in two days' time at eight o'clock in the morning. He told me his name was Brendan, and then added that he didn't know Kelly or anyone else in Rostrevor and not to go telling anyone about him, just say it was another punter who needed some roadside help. He then became really serious and looked straight at me. Then he said that there was to be no talk, no gossip. We are to meet in two weeks. He gave me five pounds for petrol."

"What do you think?" blurted Barney, and he looked at Declan who was now standing beside Barney's car. Declan narrowed his eyes, and slipped down onto his hips as if he was going to jump like a frog.

"If this situation is what I think it is, it will change our lives for good, and make us the heroes that we really are," whispered Declan, not looking up from his position.

The two did not go out during the two weeks, kept to themselves and met after work to walk and talk, always on the move, never stopping until they both got home.

Both were now committed, but scared to death, and withdrawn to their own thoughts and dreams.

Two weeks later both were on the road to the lay-by near to the farm, but as they approached and pulled into the drive, there was no sign of Brendan. Instead, a very old man with a trilby hat pulled down over long grey hair was sat on an old roadside bench. He was dressed like a traveller, with a waistcoat and spotted kerchief tied in a knot around his neck.

They sat in the car and waited, not knowing what to do. The old man was not moving and did not pose a threat and just stared ahead without turning his head. This unnerved them because with him sitting close by, it may put Brendan, if he was nearby, on alert.

Barney broke the deadlock and opened the door, as he thought that this was wasting time and he needed to be positive. If necessary, under the circumstances he would ask the old man to move on, but he did not know how he would react.

He slowly approached, and sat on the bench beside him; the man did not move a muscle. Suddenly he said without moving his head, "Whom will yer be waiting for?"

"Brendan," said Barney.

"He is not coming, it is me that you want, so yous must take me up to the stone, as I have something to discuss with you, and your friend Declan."

Barney wasn't sure how to play this but the old man stood

up and started walking towards the boy's car. He opened the back door and got in looking especially agile for such an older-looking person.

"Just drive and do not look back, and as we go I will tell some secrets." His voice seemed threatening. There was silence for a few minutes. "If you want into the army, then there is something you guys must understand – the rules are sacrosanct. Never ever talk about the cause without knowing to whom you are talking. Follow your orders, do not make up your own. Once you have signed the pledge there is no going back. Remember, never attempt to contact your superiors, they will contact you. You may be watched wherever you are, and don't ever assume that you know the person who is doing the watching. When you start your training you will become familiarized with the Green Book and that tells you everything you need to know." The man stopped.

There was a pause and Barney said, "What's the Green Book?"

"It is a very useful document, but don't worry about that now, you'll know all about that in good time," said the man. "Turn left here up the road to the Fearons' place. You will both decide to make a new life on the mainland, but do not tell your families where you are, do not even telephone them. Your contact with friends will now cease and the details for the future will be specified in the contract. You will be sent to Liverpool in six weeks' time after a few more interviews and grooming, and be prepared for your first assignment. The mechanic of you will be trained as a pipe fitter and the builder will be trained as a pipe insulation technician. Drop me off here and you will be contacted in a few days."

The man moved from the car into the scrubland nearby and was gone.

The boys drove off without saying a word.

15TH MAY 1978

Six week later the friends were on the Belfast ferry to Heysham, then they caught a bus to Lancaster and followed instructions to a bed and breakfast and checked in.

Things were moving fast, so fast the boys felt exposed, something that they could not turn away from. They were grilled in the rights of the cause at a safe house near to the B&B.

After a time they were then instructed on the ways and means that would cause the most impact to the British Government, but were constantly reminded that they were a cell and would need to be independent, with the minimum of supervision or financial backing. They would be reminded of targets and the need to prepare a report whenever contacted to do so.

Declan and Barney only discussed the instructions in a private place. Never at the accommodation.

A lady called Mrs O'Shea ran the place, she was originally from County Mayo, a staunch republican, and her partner was called Sean; the boys found them both friendly and helpful.

What the landlady and the boys at the bed and breakfast did not know was that the IRA was about to step up its campaign, and the new boys were unknowingly going to be a part of it.

OCTOBER 1978

Two years since the end of the ceasefire, the cogs were turning within the engine of the Provisional Irish Army.

New tactics were imposed by the high command, and now emphasized the importance of small cells of agents, totally independent, working alone with only minimal contact with their superiors.

The boys were now a part of it and were required to submit

reports on a periodic basis, codes needed to be learnt and the reports would be of minimal content.

Both Declan and Barney found these reports laborious and kept them brief, only advising of basis facts, intended targets and the magnitude of impact, etc.

The 'no direct contact' rule imposed by the IRA under its latest strategy made it more difficult for British Intelligence to pinpoint contacts and collaborators. The ceasefire agreed by both parties provided thinking time, but the IRA was under no illusions that the British Government was using this as a stalling point, and any concessions offered would not be acceptable to the long-term intentions of the Irish.

At this time in Ireland, it was the lull before the storm, and these two young soldiers were being sucked into the events that were to take place over the next few years, perhaps to change history.

11

A VISIT TO THE HOMELAND

OCTOBER 1978

Whilst working in the city of Lancaster, both the Irishmen felt homesick and if it wasn't for Mrs O'Shea's homely cooking and the open house, things might have been a lot worse.

After six months at the boarding house, a note was delivered to Mrs O'Shea's, addressed to Barney – 'Meet me outside the Odeon at seven tonight as I have something for you'. The sender was not identified.

That evening Barney stood outside the cinema and it was not long after he arrived that a petite lady appeared in front of him.

They exchanged code words, and she said little other than he would be required to attend a PIRA Northern Command training session.

She gave him the written instructions and told him to destroy it immediately after he had memorized it, then she slowly walked away in the direction of the shops.

The note explained that he would travel by ferry to Heysham and then find his way to an address in County Cavan.

It gave no further details but dates to arrive and depart.

Later he met with Declan and they strolled along the streets of Lancaster discussing what the training session would involve.

Declan also wanted a part of it, but he knew that his time would come in the weeks ahead.

In the two or three years prior to the pair joining the army, the PIRA had gone through a huge redevelopment of authority within the organization.

The professional leadership had always been controlled from Dublin, under the direction of the PIRA directors.

This was set to change, and it occurred during the ceasefire in the mid-1970s, when members of the six counties around the borders in the North challenged the PIRA organizing committee in Dublin, and forced a military and political overhaul.

Later in 1976, the Northern Command was formed under new leadership and it gave them a greater influence on finance, arms, and strategy.

The planning of campaigns was carried out without reference to the army council.

This led to the establishment of commando units, trained on the same basis as the British, with the same stringent and arduous training techniques.

The units were based on ten or less men and whilst in training were expected to live off the land scavenging wherever and whenever.

These manoeuvres could last for over a week, and were usually made up of men familiar with the countryside.

They normally operated at night and became skilled in the aspects of guerrilla warfare.

The new regime stopped the necessity to withdraw arms from the quartermaster, and special permission was given for commandos to be issued with a rifle, pistol and knife as a normal procedure.

It was one of these camps that Barney would attend, and it was at the start of the course that he would become familiar with the PIRA guide to warfare known as the Green Book.

Originally written in the 1950s, the book was updated in the 1970s by experienced Republican soldiers serving sentences in Long Kesh, the contents becoming much more sophisticated than were issued before, and it is an invaluable guide to all new recruits.

The contents stressed the importance of secrecy among recruits, to avoid loose talk in public, with friends or workmates.

It also stressed the importance of avoiding drinking with strangers or the over-indulgence of alcohol, as these contributed to the biggest threat to security in the Republican Army.

Barney arrived at the camp after four hours on a complex trip from Belfast, and the travelling had made him very tired.

The final pick-up by an old Ford Capri took over an hour due to the extended route that the driver had made, probably to avoid any detection by the British.

He was baffled when, after a long period without interaction, the driver suddenly stopped in the middle of the countryside and indicated that this was the point that Barney would leave the vehicle.

The car drove away from him, and as he watched it disappear amongst the tree-lined road, he looked around for a clue regarding what his next move might be.

There was no sign of people or buildings, only green fields and trees and a few cows munching on the rich emerald green grass.

He held his back straight and walked slowly along the road, but there were no clues, and he began to wonder if the driver knew what he was doing.

The day had been warm but it was now late evening and it would be dark in an hour or so.

After about fifteen minutes Barney moved behind a tree just two yards from the road and decided to wait.

Any passing traffic might find it suspicious if he was seen wandering along a road with his backpack.

As the sun slowly dropped below the horizon he began to feel cold and prepared to sleep where he was, with nowhere to go and no one to greet him.

He had packed a light blanket and with an extra sweater settled on the leeward side of the tree.

He was beginning to think that the driver had dropped him in the wrong location and, thinking of his trip home tomorrow, he dropped into slumber.

Suddenly and quite rudely he was awakened, what seemed to be a few minutes after he fell asleep, but his first sense was intense fear.

A hand was over his mouth and a sharp knife at his throat, a thick Irish voice whispered, but was clear in the still night air.

"Listen, Barney Coughlin, whatever your name is, you have plenty of work to do, and I am glad that you have had a sleep, because you will not have any more for a day or two."

Barney nodded.

"Now, my beauty, just get up. I have brought you some nice clothes to put on, and you will need to take your clothes off and put them away safely."

Barney obeyed, and in a few minutes the two men dressed in identical camouflaged clothes were making their way in the darkness across an open field.

"Tonight we have to make a hit in a crofter's old house about five miles from here." The words made Barney quiver, as it was not something that he had expected.

"Call me Pat," the man said abruptly, and then said nothing for what seemed an eternity, but it must have been only a mile of steady walking.

"This thing tonight is a training expedition and your task is to infiltrate past the two sentries posted to apprehend anyone approaching the house."

After another few minutes he continued, "They will be

armed with air rifles as you are and will shoot on sight, so you will find plastic goggles in your pocket to protect your eyes. In a few minutes I will leave you with a map, a torch and a compass. You will later be judged on your aptitude, and if it is not satisfactory, you will do it over and over again until you become the person that you will need to be."

He suddenly held Barney's arm, and signalled for him to stop.

"Your equipment is in this bag and now you are on your own. I will see you later and you will only progress onto the next stage after you have satisfied us with this one. Do you understand, my bonny lad?"

"Yes, it's clear." Barney nodded

He turned to walk away and whispered over his shoulder, "See you later, and good luck."

In a second he was gone, and the only noise was the sound of a faraway owl hooting into the night.

Barney knelt on the ground and switched on the torch. He scanned the map that Pat had given him.

'You are here', an arrow showed his whereabouts and another showed the croft.

'Your hit', the arrow identified.

Between the croft and his position were a number of vertical and horizontal roads that gave him the co-ordinates that would help his direction.

His mind was not trained in guerrilla tactics, but he was in no position to ignore his natural instincts, or his imagination that had been enhanced by the action movies that he had seen.

He tried to be in his enemy's shoes and think how they would expect him to enter the croft.

Would he use the roads or try by the wilderness of the fields?

There was a pencil in the case containing the map and he sketched the way forward.

It seemed there were no rules in this game so he tried to visualize a way to distract the guards, but how would this be possible?

Perhaps a car crash, with people wanting help, or a fake phone call from Pat telling them to change orders, but neither seemed possible.

He then remembered that he had a box of matches in his jeans – now left by the roadside. If he returned they may already have been picked up, that's if he could even find the place where the driver dropped him off.

Pat had told him that he would be judged on his aptitude, whatever happened on this exercise, so he had to create a good impression.

He walked tentatively towards the last road prior to the hill that led down to the croft at the bottom as shown on the map.

He noticed as he walked in the night stumbling over the thick grass that to his relief some of the small trees had been staked and painted white and they gave high visibility.

It wasn't long before he saw a fence profiled against the sky, running from left to right and he guessed it was the road shown on the map.

He dropped on his stomach and skidded under the bottom rail of the fence, across the road and under the second fence and peered down the slope of the field.

His eyes took some time to focus on the distance to the building at the bottom and he guessed that this was the croft with his target.

It seemed to Barney only two hundred yards from his position to the croft, and he estimated that he could run this distance up the hill in about ten minutes, but maybe faster if he was being chased.

There was no sign of the guards and he guessed that they were inside.

He turned away from the top of the hill and carefully made his way back to the other side of the road, passing under both sides of the fence.

Barney was thinking hard and he knew that he had to lure the two guards away from the croft.

He walked to the wooded area close by, and picked up a thick piece of deadwood, then loosened a pair of white poles that protected the new trees. He then found a position about a hundred yards from the road and close to undergrowth that surrounded an area of trees.

His watch showed it was just after twelve o'clock, and he thought he would wait until the early hours when the night was really quiet.

He became cold and nervous and jumped at every small noise or movement from the foliage. Then at precisely two o'clock he started his plan by steadily hammering one of the stakes into the ground.

If they decided to find out what the banging was about, he thought it would take them at least twenty to twenty-five minutes or more to climb the hill and cross the road and investigate what the noise was all about. It would not be certain where the noise was coming from and they would be wary of any ambush.

So he would bang the post slowly but constantly over fifteen minutes, stop and then walk quickly to the road and wait for his predator.

His air pistol would not be accurate at a distance, so he would need to be close to his target before shooting.

His banging sounded deafening in the still night air but he kept it up for the fifteen minutes, then stopped and jogged quickly to close to the fence at the top of the hill and lay down flat, pressing his stomach close to the ground. Then he waited.

After fifteen minutes there was nothing, so he decided to try again. This continued for another ten times and nothing had developed; he persevered, but it was becoming difficult to keep his concentration under the monotonous banging.

This continued for some time. Suddenly he saw a movement against the skyline; he stopped immediately and ran to the nearest undergrowth close by and lay prostrate on the ground. He was not in the place where he wanted to be, but not wanting to give away his position he just lay still and kept his head down. He could hear movement and guessed it was at least one of the two guards moving around looking for the cause of the noise.

Then nothing, but he kept his head down and waited further. After about two minutes he heard the same movement again but this time it was much closer.

Raising his head slightly he peered through the long grass, and there about five feet away was the shadow of a figure and his head turning from side to side. Not waiting further, he flipped onto his knees and fired his pistol at the figure.

"So you have got me, sonny boy, and now you can pass onto the croft. Good luck." Then the potential assailant turned on his heel and disappeared into the night, walking in the opposite direction of the road, and away from the croft.

Barney moved quickly to the road, to the hedge on the left side of the field, as he thought that the hedge would give him background cover against the clear night sky, and slid slowly down on his stomach stopping every few minutes for any movement from the croft.

He estimated that he was about thirty yards from a wall on the left-side of the croft, when he noticed a movement on the opposite side of the building.

Maintaining a low profile, laying as flat as he could, he focused his eyes, they locked on where he saw movement and slowly he made out the shape of a person, the face looking up the field and then to the right and left, but by his body language

Barney judged that he had not been spotted, so he did not move.

Suddenly the figure turned and walked quickly back into the croft, and with that Barney took his chance and ran fast to the nearside of the house. The 30 metres took him twenty seconds or so, and he was breathing heavily as he reached the wall.

Waiting not a second, he primed his air pistol and ran to the door just as the guard came out, and by Barney's luck, he was looking up towards the high ground. Barney fired and the man held his hands up. "Well done, my bonny boy. You have won, so have a drink and Pat will come and give you the prize."

Barney felt relieved and made his way in the dim light to the kitchen, where he found the fridge, and inside a welcome jug of cold water that he drank with gusto.

The cold drink was nice, and as it passed through his system, he felt more alive, his brain alert.

The guard did not follow him, and he thought that he was still being tested, so he sat down and thought about his next plan. After a few minutes a figure appeared at the door, and a voice that he recognized said, "What are you doing in the dark, Barney my boy? Switch the bloody light on!"

The sun woke Barney as he lay on the kitchen floor, and he struggled with his thoughts, putting together the activities of the previous night.

Warm under the blanket, his body was aching, caused by the hard stone floor. But he felt good, fully expecting to spend a few nights under the stars. He must have dozed for another hour, and when he woke raised himself and poured a glass of water and drank it all, again feeling the coldness of the liquid passing into his stomach. Feeling hungry he cut himself a slice of bread and sat down at the table to finish his breakfast.

At about nine o'clock Pat came into the kitchen with two

men, whom he introduced to Barney. They all settled around the table, with Pat sitting at the head with the rest of the team sitting down the two sides.

His face was looking particularly stern, and Barney was surprised at his opening statement. "Good work last night, my friend, but now for the detail, and with my two friends, I will go through the rest of your training programme. The classroom will be anywhere and everywhere and with the help of my colleagues here, we will provide you with all the army wants you to know. There will be a further five trainees who will join us in the next hour. In the meantime, go for a walk and read this manual; it will provide you with a good grounding."

Pat handed Barney a book that he had already heard about. "The Green Book," advised Pat, "was written many years ago but in more recent years has been updated by our friends in Long Kesh, otherwise known as the Maze Prison."

He went on talking and said sarcastically, "Somebody thought that we needed educating, so wrote this bit of literature, but it makes sense and I am sure will make a good platform for all our new talent coming in."

He and his comrades did not say another word and without further ado Pat rose and they left the room in single file. Outside the croft the others boarded an old truck and drove off in a whirl of dust and noise, with Barney left looking bemused at the door.

He strolled along the croft wall, the same one that he had run at so quickly the previous night, and simultaneously thumbed through the book that he been given by Pat.

12

THREE DAYS TO CONCENTRATE

Over the next few hours of his second day of training Barney met his fellow trainees, and he compared them with himself.

They seemed a mixed bunch, with two farmers from the west coast, a marine engineer from Belfast, an accountant from Donegal, and two plumbers from Dublin.

The lectures started in a barn behind the croft and each of his colleagues found a bale of straw to sit upon whilst their mentors prepared the week's work.

Pat started the lecture and after introducing his colleagues continued to explain the itinerary for the next three days. It seemed that each of his new friends had been given their field instructions but it was impossible to know what they were, without actually asking them, which was definitely not on the agenda.

He did find out through general discussions that four of his colleagues would be staying a day or so longer in order to carry out more exercises in order to satisfy their mentors. It seemed to Barney, that because of his success the night before, he was the star, and if this was the case he did not know whether to laugh or cry.

The hours passed and the lectures went on and on. The straw bales that they sat on made their bottoms sore.

When the military strength of the enemy was discussed it was a constant reference to the British, although almost as an afterthought other guerrilla tactics from different organizations were mentioned. They all ate at eight o'clock and drank beer together before retiring, usually at about ten o'clock.

The bed consisted of two blankets wrapped around their bodies, the mattress being the cold croft floor.

The next day continued much the same way as the previous one but the nature of the lecture changed to tactics of the enemy, technology and propaganda techniques.

The last three hours became more interesting when the bomb expert explained the fundamentals of guerrilla warfare. Another man appeared and explained different types of hand guns normally used by the army, and later discussed the devastation that long-range rifles can wreak on the enemy.

The lectures became more interesting and into the realms of the unknown when bugging devices, microphones and message scrabbling was discussed.

Sabotage and technique was the last subject of the day and took longer than expected finishing after midnight, after which they all turned into their blankets, exhausted.

Early the next day the lectures were even more intensive and Barney was no longer feeling the 'star' man thinking that it would be impossible to remember all that he had learnt on this course. Then yet another 'expert' lectured them on survival in the wild, explaining how to collect water from a barren atmosphere and how to prepare anything edible from insects to frogs. Plants, berries and leaves were explained in detail – what was good and bad, and then the conversation turned to bomb-making.

Pat suddenly put a stop on any advancement on this subject when he said, "I know that you are all on active projects at the moment and as you may read in our instruction book none of you will talk about what you are doing to anyone even to your compatriots training with you here." He went on, "I know also that you all have had some exposure to Improvised Explosive Devices (IEDs), and we will later today talk some more, but in the meantime what we need to talk about is survival."

Pat paused to emphasize the importance of what he was about to say.

"We may need to stay out somewhere wild and woolly, no electricity, no shelter and definitely no home comforts. You could find yourself on the run, but need to survive in an open field for some weeks, so you need to be in control."

He went on to explain the importance of nutritional needs. "These can be categorized into minerals, fats, fibre, carbohydrates, vitamins and proteins and each has a part to play in your survival."

Pat seemed knowledgeable on the subject and this made his lecture interesting and he got a very enthusiastic response from his trainees.

"Learn to live primitively, and adapt to your environment but if circumstances permit, make sure that you plan for your exposure. For instance always carry a multi-tool, a torch and some matches, and make a habit of carrying a selection of survival clothing in a small plastic bag."

He stressed the next instruction. "When you are about to carry out an action make sure that you concentrate on all aspects of your operation rather than the main topic, because it may save your life. And under any circumstances remember always to take a compass and if possible a map. There are other items of survival that may help you, but it will be up to you whether you take advantage of them. They are: fish hooks, scalpel, salt, plastic bag and potassium permanganate. The latter is used for purifying water, and may definitely save your life."

Pat continued for another hour and he covered lighting a fire, making camp and building a shelter that could be dismantled easily so the authorities could not distinguish the hiding place.

He explained how to confirm the position of a location at any one time, in relation to a map and compass.

"OK take five and we will continue with other things that you need to know about IED manufacture and handling."

The group stood up and stretched their legs, and Barney was straining to ask the others about their activities, but was sworn to silence and broke off to the kitchen where he brewed a cup of tea.

In exactly five minutes Pat introduced a new man by the name of Billy who he said was the explosives man who would say a thing or two about IEDs.

"First the fundamentals," explained Billy. "Almost all modern explosives are a derivative of a nitric acid base."

He went on, "Nitric acid, which is fuming, contains over 90% water and is not explosive. However," he stressed, "it is when mixed with other compounds, and this is called the 'nitrating principle'. Other chemical compounds that become explosive when mixed with nitric acid are glycerine, mercury, wheat-germ, sawdust, and starch – to say but a few. When sawdust is nitrated it becomes nitro-cellulose and is used in smokeless powder. Smokeless powder does what it says when used as a propellant, and a sound development to black powder used over the years. Mercury, for instance, when nitrated, becomes 'mercury fulminate' and is a very effective detonator."

He went on, "Nitro-glycerine is a high explosive derived from nitrating but is extremely unstable. A minor shock or change in temperature may set the device off, so I strongly recommend for all your sakes, pick one of the safer devices. For what it is worth, I will recommend the materials that can be used with some sort of assurance that they are as safe as anything when building an explosive device. Before I go into detail remember that explosives are manufactured for different purposes and when making an explosive device there are basically five stages." He paused, the first for some time.

"Power supply, possibly from alkaline batteries. Switch to trigger the device, possibly by an alarm clock or remote control. Detonator, normally a smaller explosive device than the main one, and in fact sets off the big one. Main charge. Container, or shaped charge, that directs the blast. The power supplies energy to the trigger that sets off the detonator and starts the chain of explosion. The detonator explodes thus providing energy for the main explosive and produces high-pressure shock waves. I normally use a common fertilizer for the main charge, and ANNM (ammonium nitrate and nitro-methane). One of my first devices was made up from sodium chloride, potassium chlorate of equal quantity and 20% potassium permanganate and it was successful." He seemed smug as he said this!

"Obviously the purer the ammonium nitrate the less booster and blasting cap is required. I will give you each a handbook on the subject and just be careful."

About two hours later the lecture was finished and as Barney ambled to the exit he noticed that his bag had returned from under an oak tree.

Each of the trainees left at hourly intervals and Barney was the third to go.

The destinations where the others were dropped off, he never found out, but he did know that his drop-off point was the Clandeboye golf club just south of Belfast. He knew the area and made for the bus stop where he could find his way back more easily to the ferry.

He was tempted to go and visit home as he was only about an hour away and it would be great to see his friends, family and Bridget. After some careful thought he knew that this was not possible under the terms of his contract with the army.

Feeling very sad at the thought of his home, he boarded the first stage of the bus trip back to the ferry and his digs in Lancaster.

13

THE IRISH TRAVEL TO SITE

WINTER 1978

The design and construction managers' offices became busier as the job progressed, and as more supervisors crowded into the area, the more the floor became muddy from boots, and the desks full of drawings and plans.

The site grew and it became like a London railway station, busy and noisy and almost impossible to walk through without hassle. The more people, the more attention they needed, constantly searching for information, drawings and instructions.

The process site was still at the ground preparation stage, and access to the site was difficult. Wagons carrying steel rods, and concrete tankers, and the incessant noise of pile-driving machines made the whole process area a complex area to move about. Larger foundations require a lot of preparation and handwork by the workers, and with the large heavy wagons carrying the ready-made cement the area was difficult to navigate and dangerous.

After the earth is levelled and marked out the piling team move in. Heavy pile machines that drive poles into the ground are the anchor for the foundations, these the base for the heavy structures that will stand on them. The piling machines are cumbersome and are excessively noisy and the monotonous sound of the thud as they hammer the rods into the ground is especially distracting. Once the piles have been driven, they are filled with concrete and left to set for seventy-two hours. Steel re-enforcement is prepared and wired into position after the piles are installed. Then cement is poured to create the main foundations, and the curing of these can take up to three days.

All the major steel structures bound for Sullom Voe were fabricated on the mainland, and after transportation to the Shetland site were then fitted together like a huge Lego set. Steel structures at the terminal were split into two categories, PAU (pre-assembled units) and PAR (pre-assembled pipe racks).

The PAUs could weigh up to 1,000 tons with the PARs weighing around 250 tons.

Because of the weight, more than a normal crane limit, the modules at the mainland yards when loaded out were skidded using rails and pads onto the barge, then transported by sea to the terminal. At Sullom Voe the modules were offloaded the same way, transported by multi-wheeled vehicles to the site and then jacked down onto their foundations

The estimated time of arrival dates were continually updated from information received from the fabrication yard planners, and any changes updated into the schedule.

If the planning got it wrong it would result in chaos.

OCTOBER 1978

Declan and Barney had stayed with Mrs O'Shea for almost six months and in October they were notified that they would need to move to the second stage.

The note was to be delivered by a female courier and she was to provide them with a place and time for the briefing – once the location was confirmed the briefing would be carried out by a senior man.

They were both now extremely excited and as all their training and anticipation would now be fulfilled, they could not wait to get on the move and have some fun. Declan, however, had not yet been formally trained, and although the main courses had been set up on a number of occasions, they had not taken place due to changes of plan and unavailability of the facilities. The contact time to rendezvous with the courier was arranged; the meeting was to be in the new shopping mall in Lancaster on a seat next to a McDonald's.

The instructions were explicit and they would sit on the rest benches opposite the take-away and wait for contact to be made by a woman wearing a red scarf. She would leave a package on the seat next to them giving them money, maps and precise instructions. Whenever written instructions were given, the PIRA normally used a female for courier services.

The two received their orders in a package on 12th October 1978, from the same source as previously.

The start of the note in the package read:

Travel to Sullom Voe.
Work arranged with the site contractors.

They were informed that Barney would work with a company mostly associated with the power plant, and Declan with another that specialized in insulation both within the area of the process plot and the power plant.

They were advised that the first three months would be familiarization with the site, and carrying out assisting activities whenever required. It was above all absolutely necessary to build up a good relationship with employers and workmates alike.

At the base of the note given to them in the package was a chilling instruction:

Target is the destruction of all or part of the celebrations that are due to take place at the opening ceremony, possibly in late 1980. Major casualties are to be expected in this attack and the assassination of the main dignitary the prime target.

The details of the trip were received by personal delivery the following day, and the itinerary read as follows:

Train to Glasgow.
Fly Dan-Air to Sumburgh.
Construction companies expect you to report at the camp reception.

Both the boys were nervous, and held back as long as possible before Declan stammered, "What the fuck have we let ourselves in for?"

"It is for the cause, Declan, and just think of our persecution by those bastards over the years. Now is our time."

"You're right and it is our duty to do the business, and we will go down in history dead or alive."

"Who will be the dignitary we have to assassinate?" asked Barney.

"Aw it will be the Prime Minister or one of the bloody Cabinet," said Declan. "But it doesn't matter; whoever it is we will do the job. We need to discuss the timing, the position of impact and the type," added Declan. "And I hope the men in charge tell us what they want, because we need something to go on."

"Have yer the details of travel?" asked Barney. "And make sure that we split before we arrive. Just remember the meeting points and the time that we will rendezvous." Barney was feeling irritable.

"They tell me that the construction site at the Voe is vast with over five thousand people; it may be difficult to meet without others noticing," said Declan.

"OK but we need to find a meeting point, and stick to it."

"The instructor said we must join the same clubs, so that we will come into contact normally. But as you know, Declan, I was a boxer, so I hope to get a bit of training whilst I'm there," he added.

Declan thought that Barney was trying to lure him into the gym.

"If you think I am going to join you and get my brains knocked out then have another think," Declan raised his voice.

He continued his rant, "We are not travelling to the Shetland Islands for that sort of thing so please focus and concentrate on the job in hand."

He added, "Seamus the army instructor told us to expect to be contacted for receiving the device materials."

Barney tried to cool the situation by adding something of relevance.

"And we need a place to make the bloody contraption, and not blow ourselves up in the meantime." Barney had his say.

Glasgow was dark when they arrived, and they made their way to different hotels, Barney to a hostel, and Declan to a bed and breakfast near to Central station. The budgie was due for departure the next day at eight o'clock, and they were to be sure to arrive in plenty of time for take-off and then the pressure would be on them both.

Barney rose early and joined Declan at the bed and breakfast; they were now both nervous, it was difficult to retain this and they both spoke in whispers.

They had paid for the rooms the night before and before heading to the airport, sat on the bed and made up an itinerary of actions that they needed to focus on.

They each voiced them, and made mental notes before igniting the paper with a match.

The events on that paper were:

- The date on the top of the paper read October 12th 1978.
- Familiarize layout of camp and site
- Prepare a selection of locations
- Establish place for manufacture of devices
- Confirm receptacles to be used in manufacture
- Confirm size of incendiary device and type of fuse
- Confirm location
- Possible targets
- Confirm exit strategy
- Establish expected casualties
- Confirm the principle VIP(s) and maximum for assassination

14

AT THE VOE

Declan and Barney had reached the airport of Sumburgh on the south tip of the island. The monotonous bus ride from the airport to the Toft camp was enlightened only by the wildlife on view. The land was flat and barren with only a few trees, and these bent double by the merciless winds forever blowing across the land.

"Does the fucking wind do this to the trees?" asked Barney, who was amazed at the shape of the trees bent like old men.

Declan remained silent and his thoughts were ahead of him.

A voice from a gaunt looking man sitting in the opposite seat broke the silence; the only other noise was the sound of the engine of the bus, its steady drone sending most of the passengers to sleep. The man had bushy hair, looking like it had never been combed, a moustache to match, but his thin and gaunt face hidden behind the hair made him appear a Rasputin-type character.

His voice was however very gentle, which almost hid his thick Glaswegian accent.

"Is this the first time yer boys are here on the island?"

"Yes," said Barney being the nearest person to the voice, being careful in selecting his words in order not to give any clues where they came from.

"Yer from Belfast then?" asked the Scotsman.

"Yes we are, but couldn't find much work after getting laid off at Harland and Woolf, you know, the shipyard," answered Barney. "That's where I worked but I am not sure where my colleague here worked as I have just met him."

"Aye, I worked there," said the man and much to the relief of both the Irishmen, carried on his conversation. "Aye, the wind is always blowing here and blows the hardest that I have ever seen," said the man. And he added, "It rains almost every day."

The hairy man continued, feeling that his advice was being received gladly. "The earth is peat and very acidic, and with the strong winds here the trees fall over and have little chance to grow. You may know," added the man, "that the peat is combustible and the locals have used it for years as a heating and cooking medium," he said.

Just at that moment Declan, who had been looking out of the window gave a yelp. "Look at that!" Their eyes followed his gaze.

A small sheep, idly grazing in the barren fields, was seen being plucked up and carried away by a huge black bird with an amazingly wide wingspan. The bird was under a heavy burden, and flight seemed difficult, as he seemed not to be making much altitude.

"That is a black-hooded crow," informed the man. Showing a sensitive nature to his character he added, "I suppose it is the circle of life, but I still feel sorry for the small sheep; after all, he was doing nothing to deserve that."

Barney had his own opinions on the type of bird and put it more down to an osprey, but that was of little importance under the current situation. It was also of little importance to the sheep, as it soared into the air and surely did not care what type of bird was to have him for dinner.

Slowly the bird changed direction and together with its prey clasped tightly, started to make altitude, rising high into the sky; the direction was the small hills beyond.

This seemed to end the conversation and the coach remained in silence until it pulled into the gateway and stopped outside a temporary building. The passengers in the bus peered out of the windows of the bus and saw what looked like a temporary warehouse.

"This is the Voe reception, and it is here where the clerk will know all about you and where you will stay for the next three weeks," advised the gaunt man. "And by the way, you will need to join the bloody social club, otherwise yer canna get a drink." He laughed as he stood up, picked his bag from storage and headed for the front of the bus.

The Irishmen waited until last when Barney whispered, "Remember we are not close friends but worked at Harland and Woolf, but not together." He paused then added, "No contact unless necessary and remember how to contact me for meetings and emergencies." His voice tailed off and it seemed that the leader of the two had been nominated.

Declan found himself in G block, room number 4, and Barney was in H block some way from his friend.

Barney had been fixed up with a piping contractor under the auspices of the main contractor and his work was to be associated with the piping within the power station complex.

Declan had secured a job with a company based in the north-east of England, a sub-contractor, and his work was to be insulating equipment and pipes.

The first thing both had to do was to map out the accommodation complex and find places they could meet during their leave rotation period.

They had decided that meeting places would never be arranged in the same location so Barney had took it on himself to create a cycle of times and places for both of them. It was agreed between them that times and dates for meets must be flexible and if necessary a phone call and a simple code would clarify the situation.

Telephoning did however produce a risk, so the timings of such calls were restricted to lunch and dinner breaks when both had access to site telephones.

They confirmed their targets for carrying out the main activities and made the end of 1979 the date when they would detonate their first device. As a security contingency, they decided that mainland Britain was the best place; the precise location was yet to be agreed.

As Barney was already trained in weaponry, he would construct the main device, however at their first trial runs they would detonate a much smaller device for practicalities. The smaller incendiary device would be based on about ten pounds of main charge. The trial would need to be carried out when both were on leave rotation and their intention was to set it off below ground for safety and acoustic reasons.

As yet the army had not contacted them with any specific orders and the instructions for travel and recruitment had been carried out by telephone and correspondence with packages posted or couriered to them directly. Although Barney had been the one trained in the manufacture of explosives, both remained naive in real terms.

With this lack of experience, both were nervous of the outcome and the unimaginable consequences if anything went wrong.

During the next few weeks both men turned up for work and acted as model construction men. Although naive and having a poor experience of the work to be done on this huge scale, they learned quickly and both were well liked by the other workers.

Barney had a time-served apprenticeship as a mechanic, but

he had never worked on piping until he joined the army and attended a short training course. Later he gained experience with a sympathetic pipe fabrication contractor near Derry and earned some money during his training period.

Even with the few weeks' experience during training it wasn't enough time for him to carry the job as a skilled pipe fitter. He had been taken on by his employer as a pipe fitter's mate, and by working with the tradesmen on the terminal, he quickly learnt the skills required. His sheer enthusiasm gained the respect of the other fitters and welders close to him.

For him to work in the power station, with its huge boilers hanging on the impressive structural beams and columns, was a long way from his town of Rostrevor. The size of the boilers was one thing but the miles and miles of pipework seemed like a hall full of spaghetti. Scaffolding was everywhere and this restricted movement around the work area and he found it practically impossible to carry out his own piping duties.

Most of his colleagues were travelling men, and had extremely interesting lives. Some of the older guys on site had made their mark in life previously, others had made money, but had not survived the test of time, and now they reverted back to their original skills.

Declan had found work as an insulator with a company called Inc. Insulation, a smaller sub-contractor under the management of the main construction contractor. It was dirty work and involved covering a pipe that reduces heat loss.

Declan took to the work as a duck to water and often told his friends that he liked the work so much that he would work for nothing.

All meals were provided free with a choice of dinner in the evening. They both loved the life, but were being pushed from time to time by their army contact. Their superiors wanted to know progress and the date of intended action and conditions.

The messages came through the site telephone and were always preceded by a code name that needed a pre-arranged answer.

The contact informed them that other cells were also operating within the terminal complex.

One day in November 1979 Declan left a note under Barney's door in his accommodation block and suggested a meeting during the following day. They arranged to meet in a camp common hall in the Toft camp. This was used as a utility kitchen in the evening for the bears – a nickname for the workers – who needed to cook for themselves, or just to meet and relax as an alternative to the bars.

The layout consisted of a common room, kitchen, two toilets and two small rooms for meetings and one of these was fitted with a television. The kitchen was an extension of the common room and was separated by a curtain. Between the kitchen and the common room stood a pair of one-arm bandits, part of the money-making mechanism for the social club.

During the day, they were never used and generally thought of as out of bounds by the workers.

The two had met before, but it was only catch-up discussions and spreading the news in general. It seems that at this time both were content with their lot, and making good money, and had a good social life.

However, this time Declan appeared agitated, his face strained and his mouth tightly shut. "In the top meeting room, the one without the telly," whispered Declan.

Barney shut the door and they both sat down, and in silence waited until there was no sound either from them or from outside.

Declan broke the silence. "If somebody comes in, I have come to tell you some sad news from headquarters. And he added quickly, "I have got permission from my foreman for this, so it must not take more than half an hour."

Barney spoke for the first time. "What the fuck's up, Declan? I have never seen you like this before!"

"We have been here for over six bloody months, so we have, Barney, and no plans!"

Declan added showing distain, "The army has advised me that we should be ready for August next year. This bloody lot here at Sullom Voe plan to open the terminal in early 1981. And they expect the Secretary of State for Scotland to be the main man. Our leaders want a big bang, and if it takes victims then so be it."

"If they want a big bang then we will give it to them." Barney nodded as he said it.

Declan continued his rant, "The impact required is extensive damage or death or both, but they want to be advised regarding our intentions. Tonight is 5th November and the stupid English bastards will be celebrating Guy Fawkes tonight. Can you imagine the mentality of the Brits burning some poor guy's effigy on a bonfire for a slight infringement to the State four hundred years ago? Heathen bastards."

"Was he Irish?" asked Barney.

"No bloody way, but he might have made a good Irish soldier, with a name like Fawkes; anyway he fucked up, so we don't wanna be associated with him. If we get caught they may do the same fucking thing to us as they did to Fawkes, Barney, so make sure that the bloody bomb goes off. Now we have got to start building our plans and getting the apparatus built."

"What method are we going to use?" asked Barney.

Declan became extremely serious, and crossed himself as he prepared his next few sentences. "Initially build a twenty-pound bomb and test it before preparing something bigger."

"How much bigger?" asked Barney.

"Say three hundred pounds," was the answer.

Declan whistled then clarified the specification, "Maximum

confinement to ensure optimal detonation. Mechanical timer and firing system. Ammonium nitrate to be used as the main explosive. Laboratory equipment will be dispatched soonest. Target – main opening ceremony. Location – to be clarified. Impact – maximum and no ceiling. Any questions?" asked Declan.

"When do we receive the equipment and when do we start?" asked Barney.

"By the end of 1979 we will start work, and the preparation work that is necessary will be done in an old crofter's cottage in Brae. The property has already been acquired and the rent paid a year in advance, with the location remote enough for us to come and go as we please, without arousing suspicion. However, we must always arrive by Land Rover, or the type of working vehicle that does not attract attention, and we should never be seen to be walking. It will be necessary to run the device trials on the mainland, purely for security purposes, with the bulk of supplies sent by post." Declan paused for a moment, and his forehead looked lined with worry as he said, "I think it will be in everyone's interest that we carry out our trials just with a small charge, say five pounds for the main charge, just to see what sort of bang it will make. I want to know what to expect." Declan then held his hands in the air. "Enough, my friend, time is up, we must move on."

He sighed and staring at Barney added, "Barney, my friend, we must keep concentration on the task ahead and never let this slip away from our thoughts, even for a minute; keep focused all the time."

AN UNEXPECTED MOVE

Declan's responsibilities in the workplace expanded with his reliability and dedication to the work, his management having trust in his ability, and as a result he was asked to represent his company inspecting the fabricated works on the mainland before they were transported to site.

He advised Barney, "I have been asked to work in the yards on the mainland, so will only be here for short periods until the things are actually delivered to site. Is that all right with you? I trust you can manage."

"That's not a problem, I have lots to do, and we can keep in touch by telephone if necessary," answered Barney.

Declan was now missing his girlfriend and was now disappointed in the way they had parted, but life goes on and he had important things to achieve.

"This meeting is finished, and I will advise you in due course of the next one. Not a word to anyone, and be prepared to have the trials start sometime in mid-1980 or earlier with a small device."

Declan left the room silently, looking casually both ways as he walked quickly to his vehicle. After a few moments, Barney followed, and then both were gone.

15

BOYS AND MEN

SUMMER 1978

After taking the job, Martin found himself working in the office with an interesting person by the name of Geoff de-Kok.

He had persuaded de-Kok to stay on the project after he had arrived and this proved a good move although he did have reservations. Geoff's technical attributes were not in question but it was more his swashbuckling character that was. A civil engineer by profession, he had gained little knowledge of the black trades that were starting to get busy on site.

Both Martin and Geoff got along tremendously well, and it was the former who had insisted that his friend stay on after he was made the manager, rather than depart to another building site. Black trades were associated with structural, mechanical and piping and at this time Geoff had little knowledge of this type of work, his previous experience being more associated with buildings. Growing up in a wealthy family, de-Kok had gone to private school, and throughout his life he retained that 'plum in the mouth' accent – it was totally out of place on a construction site. Absolutely wild and intelligent to boot, he lived life to the full. He was in his mid-thirties and divorced.

Recently he had met an equally up-market girl and they intended to marry, but he had never met her parents, and this puzzled him; he confided to Martin that it was like he was not worthy.

After a game of squash one day Martin had once more beaten his friend and they sat in the bar with a long cold drink. Geoff opened the conversation, "Don't know how you did that, old boy, but you always get the bloody nod, but someday I will thrash you solid. You know, Martin, I have been invited to meet Ingrid's parents next week. The problem is that she knows what I am like and I have been warned that if I do not behave myself and give a bad impression I might as well say goodbye to any marriage arrangements. Bloody influential these parents, and her father is a retired civil servant. Got to stay out of trouble on the day, as I have promised sincerely that I will be a good boy!"

Martin nodded and then changed the subject, as he wasn't sure that Geoff could ever be a good boy.

An incident had occurred that involved Geoff before Martin arrived on site, and this had become common knowledge, to all but Martin, and he wanted to know more.

Martin asked his friend about it.

Geoff explained that in his old public school days, he had attained a gift for fly fishing, so he decided to give it a try in the small lakes or pools that existed on top of the local hills.

With the weekends always busy, the best time and only time that he could fish was at night.

One particular evening he decided to give it a try.

Geoff explained that the lakes were stacked with fish, the only drawback was driving the old Land Rover along lonely and winding lanes between the peat bogs to the lakes that he said were 'full of trout'.

"Yes, old boy, that was a bit lucky, damned lucky."

He continued almost as if the subject was not worth the conversation, but Martin egged him on.

"The hills were difficult to navigate, but I managed to find some good pools, and even caught some small fish.

"You know, old boy, that fly fishing is an art, delicate and articulate and needs thought and preparation."

He went on, "The fly that is used needs to merge in with the local elements.

"The fly bait used will be either imitative or attractive, and the method of operation is either dry or wet fly. Basically the dry fly floats although the other types of fly settle below the surface."

He added, "The guys at work advised me the best thing to do for night fishing would be below water because of the poor light, but I found more success using a fly and the clear moon on the night helped me.

"The problem was the return journey, as it was bloody dark and I had forgot the time and then it was past one in the morning. On the way back the roads were a bit winding, you know, and the old Land Rover could not take one of the corners, and I landed up in the bloody bog and sank down to the axles. Bloody lucky it did not turn over otherwise it may have been curtains; you know, if the doors had been trapped by the bog and water seeping in, I would have bloody well drowned. After I pulled myself from the vehicle and trudged through the peat to the road I didn't have a clue where I was but started walking up the hill, and it felt like I was walking nowhere. And do you know what? At the top of this hill I came across a magnificent building with all sorts of apparatus hooked on the roof, almost like a Christmas tree. There was no sound or lights but I rang the bell and suddenly the whole bloody night was lit up by lights and about half a dozen larger than life guys in boiler suits stood before me. It appeared that I had stumbled on an American tracking station, but the guys were really spiffing to get out of their beds and haul the bloody Land Rover from the bog. Actually they used the company tractor to do the work and rigged up lights and all sorts; it was mighty impressive. Got home OK but a bit tired the next day."

"That sounds exciting, so let's go fishing tonight, but I will drive," added Martin.

Martin thought that even with this man 'lightning will not strike in the same place twice'.

"You know," said Geoff, as they were leaving the office later that evening, "we must get a game of golf down in Lerwick. I know that it always rains in this place but on Saturday let's make an effort, put the old waterproofs on and have a round."

That sounded a good idea at the time, but even then Martin wondered what he was letting himself in for.

THE SITUATION IS IN THE BEST HANDS – JANUARY 1979

The project manager of the design and construction company was an old sea chief engineer called Rob McKenzie, and the general opinion of the team was that he had similarities to the cartoon character Popeye. He was a short man who always seemed to be sucking on a pipe, and muttering obscenities under his breath. His eyes were dark and shrouded by thick bushy eyebrows, and a heavy black beard.

Although he had a broad Scottish accent, he lived in a house in Brighton with his wife and dogs. Martin thought that he was typical of an ex-seagoing engineer, the type that have been at sea for too long, and the mind diminished through drink.

It was difficult for most people to understand the man's gruff voice, his conversation often phrased in monosyllables, and hidden under a thick accent, and he soon got the nickname of Black Rob.

The assistant to Black Rob was a tall studious man called Fred

Phillips. Well dressed, always with collar and tie, his hair carefully groomed, he was a picture of excellence. He was a no nonsense person with a stern outlook and direct management approach.

A few weeks into the New Year, Black Rob went on holiday for a two-week break and left Fred in charge of the management team with Martin to assist him. The two weeks went quickly and the organization improved somewhat, with the production progressing well and liaison with the client going smoothly. However, all of this good work did not impress Black Rob when he returned to site.

He strode into the planning office and puffing at his pipe, gritting the stem with his teeth, still managing to sound loud, he gruffly shouted through gritted teeth, "You, in my office now," and he pointed to Fred. "And get yer man Valeron as well; we might as well have a double hanging."

Fred called up Martin who was on site at the time and asked him to come immediately to the manager's office where he would meet him.

When Martin reached the office he noticed that two chairs were positioned in the middle of the large office. Fred was sitting on one of the two chairs in the middle and Rob was circulating him still puffing heavily on his pipe.

"Sit down, my boy," uttered Rob in a gruff voice, "and shut and lock the door behind you."

These were new offices on top of the process site, with views over the whole of the construction site. However, on this day the curtains were drawn.

"Now you are both seated comfortably, let's start."

Rob took another two puffs from his pipe.

"OK let's get in the flavour of things before we go any further," said Rob sarcastically. "Let us imagine a huge cesspit in the middle of this room."

Both Fred and Martin were trying to figure out what Rob was trying to say.

"The cesspit," added Rob, "is filled with excrement, and some faeces are floating on the top whilst others are circulating from the top to the bottom. Others," he went on, "sink to the bottom and do not come up. These faeces remind me of the likes of us." Rob was now in full stride. "The faeces that stay at the top are shot at by the farmer with his shotgun, and are blown to smithereens, whilst the others that dive to the bottom are safe and survive the gun of the farmer."

He took the pipe from his mouth and sneered at the two men sitting.

"You two are the turds that stay on the top and are blown from the water, whilst I represent the ones that dive to the bottom and survive. Now just remember that whilst you are in your offices working, and when I go away again, do not change things, otherwise you both may be blown out of the water. Now both of you bugger off."

Martin looked at Fred to say something, but Fred whispered, "We will talk later." They both left the office.

Three weeks after this incident Fred entered Martin's office and whispered to him that Rob was leaving, and was to be replaced by Mike McSwain.

"Black Rob was sacked?"

His blame tactics and methods of management were slowing progress.

The exchange was carried out swiftly and Rob left for greener fields, with Martin and Fred both left to recount this experience many times.

16

BEHIND SCHEDULE
–AN ALTERNATIVE

SEPTEMBER 1978

The village at Sullom Voe was laid on December 1976 and opened in May 1978. Workers were originally flown into Sumburgh, and then travelled the two-hour journey by bus to the reception at the accommodation camp. The upgraded airport was to be named Scatsca and the new transit time for airport to site was expected to be only fifteen minutes.

Scatsca became operational in July 1978 and the budgie pilots became everyone's heroes, flying in very difficult conditions. The bears (working men) had many a white-knuckle trip into the airport with the airplane inching its way down through the fog and mist, when suddenly at a position of almost no return, the pilot brought up the nose and with throttles blazing headed skywards, to try again a few moments later.

In 1978 the operator was concerned that the construction was behind schedule and with the accommodation full, it was necessary to increase the workforce.

As a compromise the operator leased two passenger ships that were mobilized to act as additional accommodation extending the beds for around a thousand workers.

The first scheduled to arrive was the MV *Rangatira*, a New

Zealand ferry that once operated between the North and South Islands. The second to mobilize would be the Swedish cruise liner *Stena Baltica,* an up-market version of the former.

Both arrived and were operational by early 1979.

ENTERTAINMENT FOR THE BEARS

As Martin walked back to his accommodation it was clear that the spare time experienced by the men was a tremendous opportunity for his boxing plans. Providing he could harness together all the aspects that would make this thing work, the show would almost certainly be a success.

It was clear in the history of large remote construction sites that where camp facilities existed, then some sort of entertainment was required – preferably not directly related to either alcohol or the opposite sex. Bars were built on these sites in order that men could let their hair down and often the best form of entertainment that was close to their heart was some sort of combat.

The management realized that workers living away from home needed entertainment and a boxing show was the easiest way out. Having women on construction camps can cause trouble – mainly causing the men to be late to work.

Martin had experience of these problems from another site. On this vocation he was acting within the scope of project manager, his job was to ensure progress was maintained as planned and any deviation from this was to be reported to the client together with full recovery proposals.

This particular camp was on the west coast of South Africa and the men on site were showing signs of frustration. Some 'working' girls had found the camp, and were trying to tout for business. Initially the management advised the press that there was no infiltration to the men's quarters, although the security officer did mention that he had seen one incident where intercourse was achieved with the male on the inside and the female on the outside.

It was explained that the act was carried out between a wire fence, the type that showed diamond-shaped patterns in the mesh of about six inches and the height of the fence was about eight feet. However, the office never fully revealed why he had allowed it to continue.

Eventually, some women infiltrated the camp. The security company treated this incident as serious and voiced their concerns to the client; the outcome was to be discussed at the next site meeting in the site's board room.

The meeting took place every Wednesday, and the agenda was released prior to the meeting. This one attracted more than the usual attendees.

At the security section of the agenda, the security officer was asked to update the meeting on the current situation, and unblushingly reported that on the last occasion three of the working girls were seen inside the male accommodation. There was a pause in proceedings and the room was still and unusually quiet just for a minute.

Director James Cecil broke the silence. "OK. Please would the planner advise the meeting on the latest overall progress and what is the plan against what has actually been achieved."

The planner advised the meeting: "Planned on average over the last three weeks 4.8% but they achieved better than planned with 5.4%, showing 0.6% improvement."

"Then what is the problem?" said the director. "Leave things as they are, and as long as the progress is above the planned then I will turn a blind eye, and at this rate the job will be finished a month earlier then we expected."

The project was completed ahead of schedule well inside the sanction target date much to the satisfaction of Cecil and his corporate business partners.

So, Martin knew it was important to keep the men happy and the boxing show may prove to be a good line of entertainment for them. Bored construction workers need pastime entertainment and to keep workers happy the client must find a way to do this. A happy worker is a productive one and the client will go to great lengths to make this situation work.

But to set up fellow workers to stand up and fight in front of friends after a hard day's work is another matter, especially if the result is losing wages due to injury.

After the initial meeting in the gym, a boxing sub-committee was formed.

With four to six thousand contractors the problem might not be to fill the hall, but how to deal with disappointed workers who could not get a ticket through the limited space available.

17

THE FIRST STEPS TO A PROMOTION

MARCH 1979

Martin settled into living and working at the terminal, and the interest with the boxing sub-committee was a good respite from using the bar or reading a book alone in one's room.

During the weekend it was good to relax and meet some of his workmates in the bar and watch sport on the television but generally he kept away.

The boxing sub-committee became an organized voice and it was not long before a show would be on; it had already attracted funds from the social committee and plans were now in hand to promote the first show from men working at the terminal.

The committee wanted to encourage a cross section of boxers to the gym, and they had already had conversations with young men from Scotland and the northern part of England.

One particular interest to them was to encourage an Irish former boxer from Newry, now working on site; his name was Barney, and he might well be an attractive proposition for the show when it was arranged.

He was young and energetic, and he would be a good representative for the Northern Island contingent on site, so it was important that they keep him informed as things developed.

On his first leave, Martin planned to travel the short journey from his home to London, and whilst he was there meet up again with George Webster, the diplomat.

After the initial meeting in Cairo some five years previously, they had kept in touch but Martin's work in Barrow made it difficult. However, on the last of these occasions, they had met up at a restaurant called Espanol in London.

He had received a call from George earlier in the day just to say he may be a few minutes late due to an extended meeting.

Arriving only slightly later than expected, George seemed in a happy mood, and after giving his friend a hug, sat down on the stool with his arms on the bar.

"Shall we sit at the table? We can order and talk without been disturbed, I have something to discuss with you outside the range of prying ears."

As they sat at the table George ordered a good bottle of red wine. When it arrived Martin noticed it was a five-year-old Rioja, the square maroon icon stamp on the back of the label stamping its aged authenticity.

"I have been so busy you cannot believe," George advised him.

Martin shrugged. "Well that's great, George, I am just cruising."

"Will you stay up in Barrow forever?" asked George, now pouring the wine.

"I travel where the wind blows; the bigger the pay cheque the faster I go," laughed Martin.

George persisted. "When it finishes, will you go overseas?"

"I would rather be overseas now, especially if it is a year or more's contract."

"Why? Because of tax?" enquired George.

"Yes, spot on; now I wonder if you were a tax collector in a life before," laughed Martin.

"Why?"

"Well, knowing things like that," answered Martin.

"Actually I was, but some years ago now," George laughed.

They ordered the main meal, avoiding a starter.

"There is one thing about work, George; I am thinking of changing jobs, in fact I have applied for a job in the Shetland Islands, with an oil company."

"That is good news for me, Martin, because I have been thinking for some time on the subject."

"What do you mean?" Martin was curious.

"Martin, look, I have been thinking things over regarding your situation, and have talked it over with my colleagues in Whitehall."

"You flatter me, mentioning me in high places."

"My organization relies on intelligence from all over the world; it cannot always come from its own staff, but often from honest to goodness travelling British businessmen." George spoke slowly, choosing his words carefully. He continued, "It is men like you, knowledgeable people who understand how the world works, and can separate the bad men from the good." He smiled and looked across at Martin.

"How do you know that I am not the bad guy?" Martin goaded.

"Because I have already checked you out."

"Is that not a little presumptuous?" Martin seemed annoyed.

"Martin, if you feel upset on my checks then I apologize, but I normally have a second sense about people, and after meeting you the checking was only a formality."

There was a long pause and they both finished the meal and sipped their wine.

"Are you MI5 or something?"

"Something like that, but I would like to ask you to help."

"In what way?"

George now sensed that he had his man. "You may be going

to a place of utmost interest to us, it is an area which could be the breeding ground for Irish terrorists, and you are in a position to see any potential risks to our security." It was a bold statement from George.

"Hold on, George, I haven't got the job yet!"

"You will, I assure you."

"And if I do?"

"You phone me with anything, it may be important or not, but whatever it is, then let me decide."

"Do I get a retainer?"

"Maybe and maybe not, but one thing that you must not do is get involved in any action or take any risks."

"That's a relief. I'm no James Bond," said Martin.

It went silent between the two, but there was a steady restaurant buzz in the background.

George broke the ice. "You will need to swear an oath, but apart from the occasional phone call there is nothing more to it."

Martin fiddled with the last of the wine in the glass and then looked up at George.

"If it's that easy then count me in," said Martin, "especially if I get a dinner and a bottle of wine every month."

George smiled and looked for the waiter. "Terrific. *La cuenta, por favor.*"

It was now May 1979 and Martin was working in the Shetland Islands, his head down he was concerned that the schedule had slipped considerably and the planned finish date may not be achieved.

Martin had the impression that the office was busier than he had ever seen it, with a lot of activity during the past few weeks, and it seemed all the wrong people were accumulating for the wrong reasons.

The client was pressurising the main contractor to demonstrate how recovery could be achieved and at what cost. It was apparent the operator was involved because every day one representative or another was in the office, continually requiring schedule recovery plans, and this interference finally came to a head one day at the weekly site meeting between the management contractor and the operator.

The meeting had proceeded with a bad attitude; it was not long before the operator made clear his intentions for controlling the prevailing situation. Mike Brearly, who acted as the operator's 'troubleshooter', explained this at the meeting. "You will be aware that the operator is not happy with the progress that has been achieved at present." He was forthright and continued in a bullying manner. "We feel that it is now necessary for us to become involved in the work and decisions that you make, in order to recover time. It is not personal and we understand that you guys are working as effectively as possible but to satisfy our business partners it is important that we become involved. During the next few weeks we will be providing you with support from one of our consultants, and he will work from an office in your block and attend any meetings that you call and have free access to any documents that he needs to read or any particular personnel he wants to interview. He will have access as a non-functionary to all meetings; in this way he can analyse and evaluate where any problems occur on an immediate basis, and can react where appropriate."

There was no response from the managing contractor's chairman Mike Tostain who just nodded and feeling fully exposed, addressed Brearly, "Have you finished?"

"No, just one more thing – our consultants name is Michael O'Byrne, he will join us on site in a week or two, and yes I have finished for now."

All those representing the managing contractor at the meeting were stunned, as this they felt was a slight on each of them personally.

Martin was in a different position, and was thinking hard, because he felt he knew a Michael O'Byrne and if it was the same person, this could be a big mistake by the client.

He was tired when he reached his accommodation and decided to sit quietly and gather his thoughts before going for dinner.

If this O'Byrne was the same person that he knew, it could spell trouble – a staunch nationalist, hot-headed and a bully! His views were so left wing that Martin felt that politically he may cause unrest, and dare he think of the security risk, he would not put it past this character.

He picked up the telephone, and dialled a London number. It rang three times.

"Hello Webster."

"George, it's me, Martin."

"Hi Martin, how is the new job? What's on your mind?"

"Probably nothing, but a new client guy is coming to site, a man called O'Byrne."

"So what, is it enough for me to worry?"

"Maybe, maybe not, and I am not sure if it is the man I think it is but he could be worth checking out."

"Thank you for advising me and rest assured I will check this out immediately."

"Thanks George, that's all. I will keep in touch."

"Fine, Martin. It was good to hear from you. Speak again soon." He rang off.

18

A DIFFERENT DIMENSION

JUNE 1979

A departure lounge at any airport is a dismal place and the serious faces of the people waiting to board the flight to Shetland showed how they felt. The holiday over for most of them, they were now returning to site to take up another three weeks of work, leaving friends and family behind.

However, like Michael O'Byrne, some were experiencing a new episode in their lives. O'Byrne had already visited the island some weeks earlier, and carried out introductions and familiarization, and this visit was to see him officially start in a position with the client's project management team.

Loudspeakers at the airport suddenly blurted out that the flight was now ready for boarding, and this would be carried out by blocks of seats at various sections of the plane, starting from the back and working to the front.

After each section boarded then the next section was called; this situation apparently improved efficiency whilst boarding and it worked well on small planes. Although a little tedious to those at the front of the plane, who had to wait until the last call, most passengers welcomed this procedure.

O'Byrne had booked near to the front, the low numbers would be last, so he remained where he was, listening for his group of numbers to be called. He waited until all the passengers had arisen before doing so himself, but just as he did so, he felt the presence of four uniformed men in close proximity.

From the back of the group appeared a man in a blue pinstriped suit; he showed his identification, then spoke in a flat tone to O'Byrne.

"Michael O'Byrne, you are under arrest for counter intelligence activities, and it is necessary for you to accompany us to the station for questioning." O'Byrne started to protest, but feeling exposed to other passengers, thought the better of it and succumbed to the officers.

The man in the suit continued, "Anything that you say will be recorded and may be used in evidence."

In just a matter of minutes he was sitting on a hard chair in the Glasgow central police station, opposite a number of police officers looking smugly down on him. The story of his recent life unfolded before him and he sat quietly amazed at the detail that was being revealed, but he said nothing and intended to say nothing as the police continued to interrogate him.

Towards the end of the day, consuming only water, another man in a suit stood before him and introduced himself as Charles Morgan, a member of the Foreign Office's band that operated outside the United Kingdom. O'Byrne soon found out that his movements in recent months had been carefully monitored.

As the story unfolded, it was apparent that O'Byrne was a double agent, working for both the Soviet Union and the Provisional Irish Republic. His connections with Dublin were well documented, and his recent visits to the Continent and some places behind the Russian borders were also noted. Particular attention was made to his most recent visits to the Bulgarian city of Sofia where he had made contact with, Morgan thought, known members of the Bulgarian secret service.

O'Byrne said nothing throughout the interview with the

exception of a mild demonstration when Morgan advised him that he was now banned from the terminal, and would not be granted permission to visit in the near future.

It was obvious that O'Byrne was an opportunist, but what the police did not know was that he had stumbled on information that may make him some serious money.

The authorities investigating this situation included Border Control, M16 and the police, and they all needed to know every detail, every accomplice, but O'Byrne was not talking.

Although the police did not know the full story, they were quickly piecing together a formidable report on him, and after this interview they expected to know all the detail that they wanted. He had become so high profile they categorized him as High Priority Risk and the time spent on his recent movements had endorsed this.

O'Byrne was no slouch and had attended Queen's College in Dublin reading Mathematics, but due to his many activities outside of his college work, he gained a second.

A bright student, his mind was already on other things and this was further fuelled by his activities in the Student Union where he was continually involved in dissident activities. He was the type who got involved in diverse thoughts of uprising and agitation, a man to de-stabilize the world.

Like most students he was of the opinion that all the wrong people governed the world, and those who did, did so for personal gain, whilst the ordinary people strived to keep the rich. Always vocal and confrontational he made more enemies then friends. His speeches were inspirational and opinions strong and these characteristics attracted a particular individual, the rebellious type.

There was an even darker side to O'Byrne, one that was portrayed in his speeches, one that attracted both the renegades but also the police. His favourite rant to those who wanted to listen was: "The only way to cause the necessary turmoil and defeat the authorities is by force – the bigger the force the better!"

His Irish roots forced him to continually raise the Irish issue, and the PIRA was aware of the power he held in debate.

That was all the police knew at the moment; they wanted the details.

JOINING THE CLUB

His left wing tendencies, that were often versed at union conferences, attracted students from other parts of the world, among these a pretty Bulgarian girl by the name Maria Andropov.

Maria was studying languages and had already graduated from Moscow's Institute of International Public Relations. She was raised in a Marxist household where freedom of life was extremely limited and the enemy was always Western Imperialism, and America the great Satan.

The Soviet Union was beginning to soften but Maria remained a solid party member, always prompt in her reports to senior officials. The KGB was grooming her for better things, and she had already attended many party seminars for her benefit and that of the party.

Her ability with languages made her valuable to the Bulgarian secret service and they had encouraged her to attend classes for political and sporting purposes. She was a black belt in judo and her political instruction made her an ambitious female party member.

Although not a beautiful woman, she had a willowy torso, long legs and stood over 2 metres in height. Extremely slim bordering on the anorexic, her eyes and mouth appeared too large for her long slim face, and her blonde hair was normally held in a ponytail or bundled high on top of her head.

She made a point of spending her leisure time attending the many university activities that involved philosophy and politics. As a member of the Student Union she became embroiled in the discussions that prevailed, but very rarely offered any true indications of her own political beliefs.

However, she became engrossed in the meetings where Michael O'Byrne made his opinions heard, and although not truly agreeable, became transfixed on his idioms, the strength of his opinion and the forceful way he got his message across.

As the audiences grew at his meetings, there was a group that had noted his political allegiance, and one of these people who liked what they heard was an elderly man by the name of Danny O'Rierdan.

As O'Byrne departed from the hall after one particular session, O'Rierdan followed quietly, matching his step, ready to approach his man at the first convenience. In the dimly lit streets outside, he called after O'Byrne.

O'Byrne stopped and waited until O'Rierdan had joined him and after a short discussion they shook hands.

They talked for about fifteen minutes, O'Byrne fidgeting with his feet as O'Rierdan did the talking. As quickly as he started talking, he stopped, shook hands and disappeared in the opposite direction from whence he had come.

A few weeks later O'Byrne was sworn in as a member of the Irish Republican Army. He wound up his time at university as agreed with his paymasters and waited for his first instruction to start his work.

After finishing her lectures for the day, Maria Andropov returned to her small house that she shared with four other students, changed into tracksuit bottoms and a loose fitting top, squeezed on her shoes and left the house for a jog around the streets of Dublin.

She normally ran for about forty-five minutes, but on this occasion it would take longer. She smiled to two of her housemates who were in the hallway as she left and entered the wet streets outside.

At the first junction she stopped at the traffic lights and waited for them to clear before crossing, but before she could do so a large black car blocked her path.

"Maria, please open the back door and get in quickly; we must have a talk." The man in the front passenger seat slid the window shut and in a swivel movement, opened the rear door to let Maria enter. She did so obediently and in a minute, with the lights now turned orange to green, the car sped away into the night.

The man in the passenger seat looked straight ahead into the night, the headlamps of the car reflecting prisms of light through the now drizzling rain.

"Not a good night to go running, Comrade Maria." The phrase was meaningless.

"What is it, Sergei? I must not be longer than an hour because my housemates may become worried and call the police." Her answer was tongue in cheek and her eyes showed a glint of mischief.

"We may need the services of the man O'Byrne; you of course know him." He already knew the answer but wanted an assurance from Maria that she understood his meaning.

"I attend his talks and have discussed some aspects over the last year or so," she clarified the situation.

"Maria, I cannot stress the importance that you become closer to him, woo him, whatever you need to do, but we will need him to, let's say, carry out an errand for us." He paused.

"Maria, we also understand that he is almost certainly now working for the Provisional Army, and may need him to advise us of certain activities that his organization is carrying out. We will drop you about a mile from where we picked you up, and expect a report from you in about a week." The car stopped.

Maria quickly exited the car and after half an hour of gentle jogging, returned to her house.

During the next few weeks Maria slowly became part of O'Byrne's life, mainly due to her searching questions at his meetings and the support that she gave him following his answers.

He reciprocated and sought her out at the end of the sessions, interested in what she had to say about her own ideals and those of the Soviet Union.

Although she was a seasoned communist, he was interested in her views regarding the oppressed people in her country, and how Russia and the Union had changed since Stalin's era.

In Moscow and cities like Sofia, in Bulgaria, the old mechanism of communism kept grinding out its propaganda.

However, in the late seventies, things were changing in Russia, and with Stalin's prisons and concentration camps being openly discussed by the media, the people were becoming restless.

In 1975 the Helsinki Accords on human rights was signed, and later in the year the physicist and dissident Andrei Sakharov received the Nobel Peace Prize.

Russia President Leonid Brezhnev assumed the additional title of Head of State and adopted a new constitution.

With fifteen years as the head of state he was not giving up his position easily, and he would never give up his communist heritage.

In the late seventies a number of deaths occurred within the Politburo, and Mikhail Gorbachev found himself climbing the political ladder faster than he could have imagined.

Gorbachev was indeed going from strength to strength and would start a chain of events that would change history within a decade.

But in 1979 Brezhnev was still in control and he would continue to be so until his death.

In 1979 Soviet troops invaded Afghanistan and installed a Moscow-based government, but the occupation was to be futile.

Maria remained staunch in her beliefs and continued to follow the instructions of her leaders, remaining totally loyal to the party.

Following one particularly long debate after Christmas in 1978 Maria was walking along a Dublin street; she had finished telling Michael of her dreams of becoming a secretary at the Politburo, and how refreshing it would be to follow the world's affairs first hand.

They walked a bit more and quite unexpectedly O'Byrne opened up to Maria on his career intentions after graduating the following year.

"I want to give my services to my country the same way as you do, Maria, but in my case it will be until the British recognize the Irish government controlling all Ireland; things will be difficult I know but I am determined."

They walked some more, and at the junction, they went separate ways. O'Byrne normally uncomfortable in the presence of women, quickly lent over and kissed Maria on the cheek.

He whispered, "I told you this because you are my closest friend and I trust that our discussion will go no further."

The difference in their heights made his action clumsy, but the intention was warm even by Michael's own standards and this action would start a closer liaison between them – exactly what her leaders wanted from her.

19

A DANGEROUS LIAISON

JANUARY 1979

Early in 1979, the weather turned very cold and wet. Maria found it difficult to raise enthusiasm to drag herself on to the streets of Dublin for exercise, but on this night she was under instructions to meet with Sergei, so she made an extra effort to prepare herself for the cold.

As she bustled through the house with her running gear she did not see any of her housemates, it saved unnecessary talk, and once outside she felt relaxed and started her jog towards the traffic lights at the end of the road. As the lights turned red, the same black limousine stopped, and the driver hooted lightly to attract Maria's attention.

Sergei was tenser than before and went straight to the point.

"I hope that our friend is well, but time is running out, and we need his help very quickly."

"How quickly, Sergei?" Maria enquired.

"We understand from our own intelligence that his organization, the Provisional Republican Army, is planning to assassinate a very important person. We understand that if this is true, it is of absolute extreme importance to us, and we want to ensure that it is carried out successfully. We need you to find out the situation and if it is true then we will 'do a deal' with the Irish."

"His organization?" Maria was inquisitive.

"We have kept him under scrutiny for some time, and he has been dealing with certain people associated with the Provisional Irish Republican Army. We also understand that he will be overseeing an important project for them when he finishes at university. We need to know the project that he will be involved with and confirmation of the person who they are planning to assassinate."

"He will not tell me easily," added Maria.

"Of course not, my dear, and we think the best way to overcome this is for him to have a little accident." Sergei went on, "It will not be fatal, but the most important thing is that you are with him and are prepared to nurse him back to fitness." Sergei was calculating the effect on Maria.

"An accident?"

"Yes, enough to make the poor man unconscious, but not kill him."

'When?" enquired Maria.

"Don't worry about that, but remember, make sure that he recovers slowly and nicely; make sure that he has every comfort, Maria."

Maria thought for a moment and then said, "I am not sure that I can provide all his desires when recovering."

"Maria, please make it happen, and by the way, offer him a chance to travel with you home to Bulgaria; he may find it interesting."

A silence followed but only for a minute and the car slowly came to a halt.

"Good luck, Maria, and remember that we are trying to get our country back on the rails."

She was about to leave the car but held back, half sitting on the seat, her long legs protruding from the car.

"Your country is not my country?" It was a question.

"Whilst Moscow is in control, Bulgaria under the same system will benefit, and whilst this process works then we both will work together," he answered like a recorded message.

She slid from the car, and not looking back, turned towards her accommodation, which was at least two miles back into Dublin. Her situation was tense and with their examinations coming up, it left little chance for Maria to have O'Byrne to herself.

O'Byrne himself was winding down from his studies, and so was his involvement with the Student Union. The meetings and debates had been reduced and Maria found it difficult not only to talk with him, but even to casually meet him. She thought of telephoning him and making a date, but that seemed too obvious a ploy and decided against it.

During the week she normally did her shopping at a local supermarket, but this particular week she changed her routine, and decided to buy her provisions a day earlier than normal and use one that was a little further away from her home and this idea made her feel better.

As she stood over the vegetable racks deciding what she wanted she suddenly became aware that by coincidence the person next to her picking his own produce was Michael O'Byrne.

He was completely absorbed with his task, unaware of the people around him flitting between food racks selecting articles at random; he was in his own bubble.

"Michael, I have just realized that it is you; what a coincidence!" she exclaimed.

Suddenly taken aback by the interruption, and gaining the reality of where he was, he seemed pleasantly surprised to see her.

"Hi, my lovely friend, it is nice to see you."

It was her turn to be taken aback; it was not like him to express his Irish charm to females so openly.

He did not stop there with idle chat but continued, quite out of context, talking nervously about his life and the importance of the next few weeks.

"You know, Maria, I have been so bloody involved with the Student Union that I have neglected my studies, so now it is catch-up time so I am trying to do some research. I know it may now be too late."

He went on, "Actually, I am so bored I fancy going out for a beer or two on Saturday, and if you are up to it, perhaps you will come along?"

Maria hesitated; she did not want to seem to be over enthusiastic.

"But anyway if you do not fancy it, then we can leave it to another time."

"No, no I need a break from my own revising, and would be glad to join you. Not sure that I can take a pint, but a few small beers would be most welcome."

"That's great. I will meet you at the junction close to where we live, and look forward to it, but must rush. See you on Saturday about seven." With that, he made his way to the tills.

Maria nervously rang the telephone number that Sergei had left for her, and the message that she left simply said, "Road-works at the junction. Be careful with him."

Saturday came quickly for Maria and she tried not to feel nervous as she met Michael at the junction. They walked and talked and she soon realized that he was completely single-minded; it seemed everything he said he was confident about and assumed he was correct.

He made no allowance for her opinions, but that did not deter her. She thought spending an extended time with him might prove difficult. They went to a couple of pubs close to each other and each had a couple of beers, him pints and her half the size.

He mentioned that he was planning a trip to England and told her that he had three interviews lined up in London.

"What do they concern?" she asked attentively.

"Oil and gas," he answered, but would not offer anything more.

A few minutes after they left the second pub, they turned right and took a shortcut across a small park. In a second it was chaos when a bunch of young, burly men charged past them shouting excitedly and waving their arms.

In a second they were gone and after the initial surprise, she laughed and then turned towards where she thought her companion was, but he had disappeared!

"Michael, Michael, where are you?" she screamed.

There was silence.

She shouted again, but this time there was a rustle and a moan from the bushes.

She ran towards the noise shouting his name, and there in the darkness she saw a shape – it was Michael! In the darkness she put a hand out to feel him, and finding his coat, pulled him towards her.

He looked towards her, her silhouette profiled against the street lights.

"Are you OK?" he moaned.

"Yes, of course I am, but what happened?" she seemed generally surprised.

"Get an ambulance," he moaned and fell back to the floor.

"Madam, he will need to stay here for observation overnight, but will need some quiet after he gets out and someone will need to change his dressings." The nurse was talking to Maria.

"When and how many times?"

"He has had a dozen or so stitches in his head and his

arm needs to be kept in a sling as it is badly bruised, so the dressing needs changed daily for five days and then he needs to revisit here."

"That's fine, sister. I will look after him until he gets back to normal."

20

A TRIP EAST

"What am I doing here, driver? This is not my address." Michael O'Byrne could hardly move a muscle due to the intense pain from his shattered ribcage, but he was obstinate and the pain had little effect on his tonsils.

"Maria, please explain to them that this is not my house," he began to screech as the invalid chair that he was in was wheeled from the ambulance.

"Michael, it will be better if I take care of you for the next week or two, and it is one of the conditions on which the hospital released you, and besides we need to talk a little," she soothed.

"Talk, about what?" He grimaced again as the chair moved towards the door to her ground floor flat.

In precisely eight minutes the two ambulance men had laid O'Byrne out on Maria's bed and softly shut the apartment door. O'Byrne stretched out in an awkward position.

He continued to stare at the ceiling and started to speak, but was stopped in his tracks by his female friend.

"Michael, now please co-operate; you will remain where you are for at least a week, when the doctor will check your progress. In the meantime I have arranged for some time off work, and will look after you, and my bed is made up in the small room next door." There was a pause. "I will be available in the night – for your medicine," she added quickly.

She then gave him the prescription painkillers and he drifted off to sleep.

In the kitchen she gently shut the door and punched a number on her telephone. "Our patient is in bed and comfortable, but I expect it will be three weeks before we can travel." She paused and listened, and then answered, "No, I haven't told him yet, but I honestly think that this will not be a problem." Another pause and she replied, "Why, because my intuition tells me that Mr O'Byrne is a man with few scruples, and he will have none when I have finished with him." After another pause, "OK, I will keep you informed of the date when we will travel, and please reserve the seats to at least Club Class travel, as my patient will still be in pain."

The line went dead and Maria put the kettle on.

After three days the pain had subsided, and it only troubled O'Byrne when he slept or moved his diaphragm, but he was beginning to regain his drive and insatiable taste for politics, complaining whenever his reading material on the subject had dried up.

Maria entered the room with some cornflakes and milk, and as soon as she came close she became aware of his negative vibe and quickly tried to neutralize the situation.

"Michael, it is time we changed your bed sheets, so brace yourself to move when I pull out the soiled sheets."

"Fuck the sheets; that doesn't matter a damn."

She placed her hand under the bottom sheet to slide it under his bottom, but as she did so, perhaps by accident and perhaps not, her hand brushed against his manhood.

He was erect either by desire or the morning need for the toilet, as she persistently held her hand close to him.

"Michael," she whispered, "this must be a sign of getting better."

He lay back against the pillow, stiffened and pushed her hand away from his body.

"Change the sheets if you have to, but I am not here for any other reason than to get on my feet, and get back to my business."

He was aloof and cold which irritated Maria, but like a professional diplomat, she continued without saying a word; she did not want to spoil her plans in any way, and she knew there were other ways of skinning a cat. She remained silent and would try Plan B later.

The next three days saw a continued improvement in him, and after a week he was moving around her apartment quite easily, although any sudden movements gave him a jolt of pain.

Their relationship had slowly grown intellectually, as she had found common ground with his politics, and had stayed up at night reading as much as she could, to familiarize herself about the situation in Ireland.

During their conversations she always tried to liken his politics with her own Marxist views, and he became sympathetic, but always finished their conversation with ways on how to solve the situation.

They always seemed dramatic and violent, but this suited Maria and she waited for a time to suggest to him her travel arrangements. She was not confident regarding his sexuality; especially after the 'under bedclothes' episode, and she had not pursued it further, instead keeping their relationship on a professional basis.

"Michael, I will need to go back to Sofia in a week or so to report to my superiors, and may I suggest that you travel with me; it would be pleasant to have your company and besides I would like to introduce you to some..." She paused. "... Important people."

He looked up and stared at her silently trying to ascertain the situation. Then picking out the parts of the conversation that most appealed to him, looked out of the window with apparent disdain.

"Important people?"

"Yes, Russian and Bulgarian people with strong political views, who want to act in the same way as you, in solving problems I mean. It could be very interesting for you."

"Maybe, OK," he said. "But only for a week. I may need to travel with a stick, as these ribs are so bloody painful!"

In Sofia a large black limousine met Maria and Michael at the airport, and whisked them away to a hotel. They checked in using their own names, having separate rooms, although they were close to each other on the fifth floor.

The old hotel, built during the old imperialist times, was fit for purpose, but it had seen better days.

On the evening of the first day they were seated in the dining room of the old hotel and were joined by another man, already known to Maria. She remained very business-like as she greeted him, and did not speak unless addressed by him.

He introduced himself as Ivan Varushkin, and his prime duty was to advise O'Byrne on what to do and where to go during his two-day stay in Sofia.

He pulled up a chair to the table and ordered drinks and a meal and the conversation flowed fairly easily despite his broken and stinted English.

After they had finished, Varushkin stood up and addressed O'Byrne, "You will be picked up at eight o'clock, and I will take you to talk with someone very interesting."

As he went to go he turned to Maria and said, "Comrade Andropov will visit her office during our visit, and will not accompany us."

He nodded and walked away.

21

A RUDE AWAKENING

MARCH 1979

"We will not, as you say, 'beat about the bush', but come directly to the point." O'Byrne sat in a high ceilinged room; at both ends were tall half doors that opened from the centre, and were the height of the room.

The room was dark and the furniture heavy; nevertheless a feeling of opulence filled the space, albeit with a cold feeling. Three men were positioned around the main table, upon which were scattered sheets of paper. Michael O'Byrne sat at the main table, and his usual confident nature seemed to have deserted him for that moment.

Two of the men sitting close to him seemed to be from the same organization; whether it was the Bulgarian secret service or the KGB was only a guess. They continued to speak to each other whilst the third man sat aloofly at the end of the table away from the rest of the party.

O'Byrne was not to know that the man at the end of the table was known as Abdullah Cavdarli, a leader of a secret organization calling itself 'The Grey Wolves'.

"Mr O'Byrne, we understand that you are part of an organization called the Provisional Irish Republican Army." O'Byrne started to object, but the lead man raised his hand. "That is no business of ours but I am leading up to a proposal that you may be interested in. Whilst studying at university you became a well-known student, a dissident known for left wing tendencies, and again may I say that this is no concern of mine other than in admiration. My name is Dmitry and I represent a similar organization as your own, and because of this I am prepared to offer you a business proposal."

"A business proposal?" asked O'Byrne.

"Before I go further, may I remind you that anything that you hear in this room will remain in this room. We represent the Bulgarian Government. Should any of our conversation be leaked, we will hold you responsible. Mr Cavdarli, the gentleman at the end of the table, is Turkish and has no direct interest in our conversation, but he wants to be aware of dates and places."

"Whatever it is will remain with me; that is my training in any case," replied O'Byrne.

"That is good. Then we must make our proposal. We understand from our own intelligence that you have agents on Shetland some three hundred miles north of Wick in Scotland. We understand that you may be intending to cause disruption at the newly built oil terminal at the opening ceremony sometime in 1980. We understand that you are planning to assassinate a very important person." He paused for a moment.

"That may be possible but I do not know the details," broke in O'Byrne.

"Mr O'Byrne, I think it plausible that you find out from your organization the details of such an operation. You see, Mr O'Byrne, it is of absolute importance to us that this action is carried out successfully, and under your PIRA's control. You see that the assassination of such a high profile dignitary would be of utmost importance to us. To ensure that the action is carried out successfully we propose that the PIRA consider our sponsorship."

"Your sponsorship?" asked O'Byrne.

"Mr O'Byrne, we will subsidize your organization with the best Soviet arms available up to approximately £1.8m."

He narrowed his eyes and peered at O'Byrne.

"To you personally we will deposit £50,000 in whatever bank account you specify."

No one spoke.

"Mr O'Byrne, your comments please."

Later that evening Michael and Maria dined silently together in the hotel dining room. She knew roughly what had been said at his meeting but decided against any conversation, the information she knew to be classified. After an uncomfortable hour sitting together without conversation both departed to their rooms early in order to catch the flight back to Berlin and for him a connection to Dublin.

She told Michael that she would travel onto Paris from Berlin, but instead had intentions of returning on the next flight back to Sofia. Unknown to O'Byrne, the meeting in Sofia had a direct relationship with other developments underway, probably as daunting as the one outlined to him but he was not to find this out until the spring of 1981, or before if the Bulgarians thought it in their favour.

Through his most recent business with the PIRA's office in Dublin, O'Byrne had been briefed on recent developments that were planned for the terminal. The most important of these was news that Her Majesty the Queen was to be the main dignitary at the opening ceremony together with her husband the Duke of Edinburgh.

It was now important that he was designated to lead the operation in Shetland currently run by two inexperienced recruits and his first task would be to visit the place and make his introductions.

He now needed cover and if he was to be assigned to Sullom

Voe then what better way than to work for the operator. His interview with the oil company must go well at all costs!

O'Byrne was a man with few scruples and outrageous ambition. He now knew that the Russian secret service was interested in the activities in the Shetland Islands and by more luck than judgment, he was now a part of it.

This became even more intriguing when O'Byrne, during the visit to Sofia, found out that the Russians, apart from their participation at the terminal, were also planning other acts of terrorism elsewhere.

Within six months O'Byrne was on board and now understood that he was in the big time. He had brokered a deal with the Russians but he now needed to have knowledge of any others and now kidded himself that he was the most dangerous agent in Europe. That was until his unscheduled appointment at Glasgow airport with MI5.

.

22

A MOVE IN THE RIGHT DIRECTION

AUGUST 1979

Declan had now been transferred to the mainland, but was becoming frustrated and impatient due to the isolation from his friends at site. Working away from the island was never planned, and the targets that he had set himself when sent to the Shetland Islands had not progressed as fast as expected. He knew that those in Dublin were not happy, and was now afraid that he may be side-stepped if things did not move faster.

The one redeeming factor was that the actual opening date was planned for late in 1980 and time was still on their side. On a personal note he was missing his companionship with Bridget, not to mention the sex, which was short but enjoyable at the time; he now knew that on a long-term basis, things may have got better but now with his involvement with the army, it would have to wait.

He felt, by leaving his friend alone on the site, Barney could become distracted and not fulfill what was required of him. However, a break did come Declan's way, when he was asked to accompany a huge fabricated pipework structure up to site. It had completed fabrication and was due to be shipped in three stages, and Declan was asked to accompany the loads during the shipping. This would allow him to check on Barney's progress and make sure he was concentrating on the main things in hand.

During the start of the transportation he rang Barney and arranged a meeting with him at the normal rendezvous point, and a time and date was agreed. Barney had found new confidence working alone and had worked hard developing the charges.

It was now an irritant to Barney that Declan was to return as he was making his own plans to prove himself as an explosives expert. "How the devil are you, my friend?" said Barney as Declan sauntered in to the meeting room.

Although both were glad to see each other, there was an aura of disdain and the initial greetings were followed by an embarrassing silence. At the same time as the two Irishmen were extending greetings to each other, Dave Osley the social club treasurer and Martin were leaving their offices to make the coin collections from the sporting machines at the various centres.

Both were now committee members of the social club acting in the capacity of treasurer and assistant and their job was to empty the cash from the machines. Their first stop was the No 2 service area, the same meeting place where Declan and Barney were now in urgent conversation.

As the Land Rover approached the hilltop, as it had done every week, they noticed a door open at the kitchen entrance.

"Let's be careful. I am sure that should be locked," said Dave.

Deftly they walked towards the machines, stopping after only a few steps as they heard raised but muffled voices.

"These guys should not be in here; it's banned during work hours," whispered David.

"Sounds like Irish accents," answered Martin keeping his voice as low as possible.

Dave smiled. "That's Barney Coughlin." But held his finger to his lips.

Both guys listened as the tone in the room became excited, and both men in the room seemed to be arguing.

"And I am fucking telling you that the target has changed and now it will be the bloody…" the voice was heard to say.

"What did he say?" whispered Martin.

But Dave shook his head.

The talking in the room was spasmodic, with the sound rising and falling.

"I couldn't make out the conversation, with the exception of the first sentence when we came in but I could have sworn he said it was the Queen." Martin looked shocked.

"Don't speculate," warned Dave, "it may get us into trouble, but do you agree that it sounded like Barney?"

"I think so, but we cannot be sure just hearing a voice, so let's leave it at that for the moment."

Dave nodded towards the door, and they both departed quietly and would return later to do what they had come for.

The experience left them cold, and they carried their thoughts secretly, however the situation appeared more serious than could be imagined, especially regarding the voice that Martin thought he had recognized.

Nobody on site would believe either of them if they reported the experience, and should this become common knowledge and the wrong people took exception, they would be in fear of their lives.

It passed through Martin's mind that this may need a call to George Webster, but decided to leave it until he had further evidence of identification.

A week later Declan said goodbye to his mate and headed back to the Hartlepool fabrication yard where he was located. He expected to return again with the second load in a week. Barney could not wait to get rid of his friend because he had plans over the next few days.

Martin lay tossing in his bed unable to sleep; his mind was not telling him the same as his heart, and he could not make a decision.

He was confident that the voice that he had heard was indeed Barney Coughlin's, but he was not absolutely certain. If he made a phone call to George Webster and it was not Barney it would be very embarrassing; he was a friend.

Martin had no one to confide in. If he was right and did nothing the consequences did not bear thinking about. He needed to confirm the evidence, he had time, and it needed to be without doubt.

The night dragged on, and he just did not want to face the world with such doubt in his mind. He needed to stay close to Barney, talk with him; he knew if he was an IRA agent, he would not disclose anything to him, and even if he did it may then be potentially dangerous.

But the situation prevailing before him was one of life and death; other innocent people were in danger. Now he was the man responsible should anything go wrong.

Before he fell asleep he had decided to visit George in London and have a chat with him, and explain his fears and concerns as soon as he could. This did not deter from Martin's own task of investigating Barney more closely.

23

BARNEY UPS THE PACE

APRIL 1979

Barney was in despair; he had worked hard in the cottage at Brae without actually proving his worth, and he now needed to be more positive. He was ready for his first live test and felt that it was better he carried this out without his friend. He wanted to stamp his mark on the camp with warning but without malice and he wanted to create a maximum scare tactic.

His first trial below ground was carried out a week earlier, and turned out successfully, his ego was at its peak and now he wanted to go up a stage and actually destroy something without hurting anyone.

He fantasized that he would be feared by Westminster and feted at home where his lone hero photo on the pub wall would be seen in the years to come. His workshop in Brae contained a number of devices in various stages of completion and he had it in mind to use one of them but had not decided where it would be.

Martin felt uncomfortable regarding the conversation in the common room, and needed the confirmation one way or another whether the voice that he'd heard was that of Barney. It was because of this doubt that his relationship with Barney was not good, and the only way to get an answer was to have a one to one with his old friend.

Martin invited Barney for a meal one Monday evening after the boxing show and the closer the time came the more nervous Martin felt.

He thought about different ways to broach the subject with Barney but could never find a way to make it sound unimportant, and by the time that Monday afternoon had come he had resolved nothing.

Martin telephoned Barney. "Can I propose that our dinner date is postponed until I move onto the *Stena*? It will be better, more relaxed and we can enjoy it."

"That's great, Martin, fantastic and I look forward to seeing you."

24

BOXING AT THE VOE

The show was scheduled for a Saturday night commencing with doors opening at seven o'clock. Everything seemed to go to plan and somehow the committee had scraped together six bouts. The last was matched the night before the show when some structural workers came up with a heavyweight to fight Martin.

The sales had gone well and all tickets were sold some exchanging hands up to ten times' face value. The main event was a ten-round contest between a smart English amateur and the older professional.

FIGHT NIGHT – APRIL 1979

At precisely eight o'clock, the tables were full with plastic glasses of beer; each one would disappear in a moment the bears sat down, they certainly would not last long.

The high majority of the thousand people crammed into the hall were mostly rough, tough construction workers, but dotted around amongst the workers included many office workers including a team of the managers from the client's team with the project director at the head of the table.

The hall looked magnificent, the ambience electric, and the waitresses immaculate. Tables were decorated with small posies and each had a place setting with the appropriate crockery and cutlery. Waitresses greeted their guests at each table introducing themselves, and all were smartly dressed, ready to bring their orders. The only items that looked out of place were the plastic glasses and water jugs. In the middle of the table was a small plate of nibbles that the attendees could munch on whilst they were waiting in between bouts.

But they were all here for the action and eager for the show to start; the anticipation seemed to excite the men, as the volume of noise in the hall was turned on.

After the first fight the floor of the hall was already awash with beer and the air filled with smoke, like London smog. The barmaids worked incessantly and were rewarded with huge tips. They were making more money for themselves in one night of boxing than they had in their monthly wage packet.

The boxing was skilful and exciting much to the delight of the crowd, with each of the bouts going the distance. The officials acted professionally with no mishaps, and the show went without trouble... so far.

At the end of the night the attendees watching the show filed out of the hall quietly and the buzz of excitement remained in the hall. The ring lights were turned off, and with them went the excitement of the night; the centre piece of the show was gone.

A few of the audience remained drinking and laughing in and around the hall so Martin and some friends decided to have a nightcap at the Hilltop, and left the hall, content that the night seemed a success.

It was about fifteen minutes before they reached their destination, and as they arrived, Vee the barmaid, seeing Martin and his entourage, hurried over to speak with them.

"Yous had better get back to the Voe hall, my likely lads, cos it seems there is one almighty fight going on with chairs and all sorts."

Vee had seen it all before but she knew that whatever was

happening in the boxing hall might cost the livelihood of the men that were fighting.

Martin did not wait for the details but moved quickly, and headed back to the auditorium closely followed by Osley and some of the others.

As they hurried towards the auditorium he talked nervously to his friend.

"You know, Dave, because of the nature of boxing, this sort of thing often happens so it is always important that the events are controlled properly, and when they are not there are plenty of kickbacks." He added angrily, "And I thought that we had done just that until this thing breaks out, and I know what the press is going to say about this in the future." He went on talking as they hurried back to the Voe. "The problem is that the camp management, after hearing of this lot, may not allow any more boxing activity. It sickens me!"

The two friends reached the hall and quickly walked past the two sets of swing doors and entered the hall. The tables around the ring area were in disarray with many chairs all over the place, and this left a gap in the table area. A group of guys were standing and another two were sitting on chairs, one holding his head. There was blood on the floor, and Martin approached one of the guys.

"What the fuck happened here?"

The guy nodded and without looking at the two inquisitors answered, "Some idiot tried to take on the guys who were left in the hall; thinks he is champion of the world. Two of the stewards returned and hauled him away."

"Who was the troublemaker?" enquired Martin.

"It was the manager or the sub-manager of the catering group. He was so pissed, his trousers were halfway down his legs and each time he threw a punch they fell down a bit more. Before the stewards got to him, he tripped over his trousers and fell on the floor."

"And that was it?" said Martin.

"Well, when he went down the guy that he was knocking ten bales of shit out of stuck the boot in and caused some of the ketchup that you can see on the floor."

As he was catching his thoughts, one of the two stewards returned.

"We have taken him home, and he seems to be behaving himself, but there were still two client guys having a drink here at the time, so I don't think it will end there."

Martin thanked him and moved away, and he murmured to Dave as they walked away. "It looks OK now, so let's get our drink, but one thing is sure, I will need to get a short report tomorrow and give it to management before anyone else gets to them."

They both walked slowly back up the hill and tried to put the world to rights as they went. They stopped at the junction where Dave would take a different path but continued talking for another hour, and by now it was two o'clock and it was time to say goodnight.

25

STENA BALTICA

MARCH 1979

The cruise ship *Stena Baltica* sailed into Sullom Voe in March 1979, and those 650 people who were lucky enough to be allotted a cabin were in clover. Martin was one of those people and moved into his cabin only three days before the show.

The conditions were unbelievable for site accommodation, with a gymnasium, a four-course buffet meal, and lounges in abundance when off duty. Visitors were granted permission to take a meal on the ship if invited by a member and with prior notice to the caterers.

The ship was moored just outside the main site gate, and access was via an extravagant gangplank, its lines curved and elegant, and for decoration the crew had hung small white marker buoys from underneath the structure.

JULY 1979

Barney had returned from his rest and recuperation period and spent his entire time on leave revising his IED techniques. But he was becoming impatient and wanted to put his knowledge to the test. After all, there was no point in knowing everything about something if your knowledge was not put to the test, and this was how Barney thought of himself now.

He spent nearly all of his spare time reading and preparing dummy devices, but he was feeling unfulfilled in his position. The action that he expected was not forthcoming fast enough, and he was confident now that he could show what he was really capable of. He had tried out a controlled explosion in a pit, with the primary device triggered by an alarm clock. He was feeling satisfied and wanted to step up a gear.

Declan on the other hand maintained his focus at all times, never wavering but he too was keen on some action, but waited patiently for the call from Dublin. Always retaining calm within himself, he was forever telling Barney to be patient and wait.

Barney kept Declan informed about his progress and the physical state of the devices that he had been building at Brae. Always tentative about the cottage being discovered, Declan kept reminding Barney of the security procedure and the necessity to be discreet when arriving and departing.

"Always be on the lookout. Never take anything for granted and never enter the cottage if you see anyone who can identify you, my friend."

"Yes, yes, I always check and no one has seen me go in the cottage yet," said Barney irritably.

However, one thing that he kept to himself and never mentioned to Declan was his plan for a live trial – no casualties planned, only damage to property, and it may be risky, but it needed to be done. He was impatient and intended to do his thing during Declan's next visit to the mainland.

Barney had not yet found a suitable target, but he was looking for the first opportunity and this was soon to come. The news that the Secretary of State was to visit the Voe made things suddenly interesting although nobody at the time knew the reasons for the visit, his intention would be a start in the right direction.

Barney could only work at weekends and evenings at the cottage, but he knew that time was not favourable; he needed to put in more hours at Brae!

He had planned for at least one test run before the real thing and if everything turned out successfully with this he would expect it to occur around the first quarter of 1980.

Because of his dedication to work, his rest time was absorbed at the cottage and he had little time to spend at the boxing gymnasium, his one other leisure time activity.

As well as maintaining his own physical fitness, Barney felt that he needed to support the boxing club. He had neglected this in recent months. It made him feel that he had let the team down. Promising Barry after a training session at the gym that he was available for the tournament, then pulling out, he had become unreliable and needed to offer them something back and at the same time, start using the club to cover his tracks.

He decided to telephone Martin, apologise and offer his services for the club's support. It would be good for the club to have an enthusiastic member and also for himself as this may give him extra cover that he would need.

If suspicions were raised concerning his whereabouts, and he was an active member of the boxing club, he could easily make the excuse that he was there at the time.

It was always busy with people coming and going and was an ideal place to hide his tracks.

"Hello, Martin, it's Barney." His hand felt wet on the handset of the telephone.

"I was just thinking about you," Martin responded.

"What about me?" Barney was now curious.

"No, nothing important, I was just wondering if we could

make our dinner date now that I am on the ship." Martin sounded casual, but the anticipation was building inside him.

"Hey, that sounds fine, whenever."

"Monday at about seven o'clock?" Martin suggested.

"Good for me, so see you then." Barney seemed buoyant.

On the Monday evening in question, Martin came down from the ship onto the gangplank and looking down, immediately saw Barney waiting below. He had left his vehicle but was standing alone near to the edge of the quayside.

He appeared preoccupied, totally absorbed by the movement of the ship between the fenders and the gangplank and did not even notice as his friend approached.

"Barney, man, what are you doing, thinking of going for a swim?"

"No," answered Barney, "just looking at the power of the sea."

They both seemed relaxed and strolled together up the gangplank and onto the ship. Barney noticed that the lighting on board was subdued and the area of the buffet and seating arrangement was much more comfortable than he was used to on the camp.

The patrons were all dressed in smart casual attire, with the crew in smart dinner dress uniform. The people who Barney met, whether he knew them or not, were curt and polite, and acknowledged each other with nods and bows.

Martin took Barney round the ship and showed him the living and mess quarters, and he seemed impressed. Whilst they were walking the decks, Martin raised the question, "Do you ever have the time to get back to camp during a working day, Barney? Or are you restricted by your company?" asked Martin.

"No," answered Barney, "nobody watches us that closely, but I do not have reason to go to camp during the day, so that never causes a problem. So why ask, do you want me to do something for you?"

"No, no," said Martin, "it's just that I thought that I heard you talking the other day when I was collecting the proceeds from the slot machines."

"Doubt it," said Barney, "although I did pass through last week to collect a mate who'd just arrived from the mainland."

"Couldn't have been you then," concluded Martin who decided to drop the matter for the moment.

They finished up with a drink in the ship's bar and Barney was suitably impressed.

"But, Barney, we have missed you, especially as we had you down to fight at the show." Martin continued to fish for information. "We had just the man you could have fought and vented some of that Irish temper!"

"I heard the show was good and would have liked to have participated but I am extremely busy at the moment, especially with some business on the mainland," answered Barney.

"By the way," remembered Martin, "I had a new guy, who visited me. He was due to start work here, but in the end did not. His name was Michael O'Byrne." Martin looked up at Barney to see if he showed any recognition of the name. "This guy is a wild man, quick tempered, an Irish temper you understand."

"How do you know him?" Barney was inquisitive.

"Oh I met him on a site in the Midlands a couple of years ago."

"Do I know him, or am I supposed to know him?" queried Barney.

"No, not especially, but I am telling you because he was Irish, and studied in Dublin." He went on, "When I first met him, I was working as a construction troubleshooter. Subsequently I was sent on a job in the middle of England. It was at the time undergoing a major shutdown. The old station needed upgrading and the work was getting behind schedule so somehow I got involved."

"What did you do to improve things?" asked Barney.

"There were many problems, so I concentrated on the three main issues that I thought were the causes. They included the low morale of the workers, the high pipe-weld repair rate and the non-existent planning and organization of the work to be done."

"So where did this Irishman come in?" Barney asked but seemed agitated on Martin's insinuation that he should know this guy O'Byrne.

"We hired one guy for weld quality and the other for project controls, the latter was the Irishman."

"OK, but what next?" Barney became impatient.

"I fired them both in the end, as both turned out unsuitable." Then Martin added the sentence that made Barney raise his eyebrows. "And to boot the Irishman was a staunch Irish Nationalist in the bargain," said Martin.

"What do you mean Nationalist?" asked Barney innocently.

"Well, an Irish Catholic, just like you," smiled Martin to himself. "I also have an Irish background as you know, Barney, but when I challenged Mr O'Byrne on a number of occasions he slapped me down."

"Was that all?" Barney enquired. "I would probably have done the same thing," he countered.

"Probably nothing and I dismissed it as sensitivity, knowing full well how some of you Irishmen feel, and I say that because my parents went through that same troubled business." He quickly went on, "They left the old country because of the difference in their religions, my father a Protestant and my mother a Catholic."

"Your mother should not have done the marriage thing," Barney advised. He added, "A mixed religion marriage is racialist. But tell me more about this guy O'Byrne."

"Not much to tell other than he was a troublemaker and a

an undesirable as far as I was concerned. I may well have been right to be concerned as I have just heard that O'Byrne has been stopped at Glasgow from boarding the plane as a high risk and is now under police questioning."

Barney broke in quickly, "Undesirable for what?"

"Apparently…" Martin hesitated.

"Apparently what?" Barney became agitated.

"Apparently for IRA activities. He did say he was bringing with him two Dublin graduates who specialized in project controls, but I don't know what has happened to them."

All sorts of thoughts flashed past through Barney's mind and the silence became embarrassing.

He finally replied, "That's bad for O'Byrne but what the fuck has that to do with me?"

"As I said, I thought that you may have known him through the Irish contingent," answered Martin.

"No, no, I haven't heard of him, but to be sure he sounds as though he was an academic anyway."

Barney then decided it was the best time to end the discussion. "It's been lovely to talk with you. I have to get up in the morning, so let's keep in touch. Bye for now."

"Before you go, mate, please make a date with me. We will have to do this again."

"That would be great," answered Barney.

"Then I will ring you at work and confirm." Martin made his way back to his cabin.

Barney was now suspicious of Martin and his involvement with the man O'Byrne.

But if it was true, what was O'Byrne doing at the terminal? Barney knew that the army strategy had changed and going into the 'long war' had adopted a new tactic of independent teams to do the dirty work; these teams were each part of special units that worked in cells.

Barney had been trained in this way, and was of a similar ilk – they had been trained in the independent team concept and were aware of how it worked. He had acknowledged this but what and how, he thought to himself, was O'Byrne up to?

Arriving back at his accommodation, he went to bed excited; he now had immediate plans for the future, not from Martin but from the opportunity he saw at the ship's side. Barney thought to himself that his first plan needed to be carried out ahead of Declan returning to site.

26

THE SULLOM VOE SOCIAL CLUB

To facilitate a social life for so many workers on an island over 100 miles north of the mainland is a challenge. Although it is the responsibility of the operator to keep the workers happy, it is a specialized activity, and one that others normally carry out.

In this case the operator provided an opportunity for individuals from each of the main contractors to set up and run the social affairs during the life of the project. Those who were involved would be elected by members and permitted by the operator to work between social club and employers on a part-time basis.

Sub-committees were set up to cover the many activities for the thousand or so people involved and the spectrum of sports concerned. The social club grew in stature and the turnover extended to nearly £2m during the peak of activity. The alcohol sold at the many bars brought in valuable funds as did the gaming machines positioned in strategic positions around the accommodation area.

The men worked hard and were generous in their spare time making the social club financially big business.

27

A DIP IN THE VOE

DECEMBER 1979

Apart from activities provided by the social club the client tried to encourage social events that involved themselves and their managing contractors. They organized ten-pin bowling competitions, hash runs, and of course the normal British pastime, darts. This type of pastime would involve members of both sexes and those who would not be involved in more active sports.

Just before Christmas in 1979, the client arranged a darts tournament between themselves and staff who worked for the design and construction manager. It was encouraged to submit teams with a mixed sex, and this brought a sense of glamour and sociability.

The operator had many female workers – some were married, some were single but a night out was always welcome in such a mundane place and each made the best of the occasion. Those single girls at the terminal usually paired up with a male sooner or later, and those married girls on a single contract sometimes did the same.

Because the men outnumbered the girls the sexual pressure was on the single-status females. Everyone knew the consequences should problems arise due to the project ban regarding co-habiting.

To make it interesting, many of the females were either girls doing some inter-country travelling, stopping over for a bit of extra cash, or career girls working for British companies and transferred to the island on a contractual basis.

The darts match that was arranged early in the spring of 1979 was to be played in the upstairs room above the famed Wellie bar. Martin was quite a good darts player, and this particular night found himself partnering an Australian girl called Lexi.

She was in the middle of her travels, but had secured a medium-term job with the managing contractor. Her travelling companion from Australia was an attractive blonde girl called Sally and they worked together.

Sally also attended the darts night but on this occasion partnered a representative called Mike Redding. An attractive female, Lexi was in her late twenties, pleasant and forthcoming, but tough as teak and would break into four-letter expletives at the blink of an eye. She took no nonsense from 'would-be' womanizers, depending on her mood at the time. However, it was rumoured on site that if she did fancy a man, then she would catch her prey by his balls and drag him off to her lair.

Martin and Lexi got on extremely well, and there was probably a mutual attraction, but neither took the chance of the first move. So as a perfect working relationship, they made a good partnership.

"How yer doing, mate?" said Lexi to her female opponent who was clearly taken aback by the proposed introduction.

"Well, I'm… I'm fine," stammered Olivia in response.

"Yer fancy your chances, do yer, mate?" teased Lexi.

"I haven't played much, but my partner Mike and I will try our level best," reasoned Olivia.

"You betcha, so let's hit it guys. Who is to throw first?"

Mike was the construction manager of the process area and deputy to the client site manager. As a confirmed bachelor, Mike was clearly not at ease with the brashness of the Australian female, and it was obvious that he was ill at ease.

"Let's toss a coin then, Martin. So, to understand the rules, each team goes for it straight away, deducting after each throw." And he added, "And of course the main thing is that to win, it is double out."

Olivia was a demure and educated young lady in her early thirties who worked for the client as a corporate lawyer. She was well travelled and had previously worked in the Middle East for the same client in the same role. She spoke quietly and correctly and when she scored fifty-five with her first throw she showed the most amazing smile and giggle to match.

The result of the match was of little importance but it seemed what was more eventful was the relationship that Martin and Olivia had struck up. After the match had finished they both moved away from the main body of people and spoke privately to each other.

They departed the bar together and as Martin left her at the steps of the bus she blurted out, "Martin, please ring me and come to dinner at my bungalow down near Brae. I share with a fellow legal adviser and she has a partner so it would be nice for you to meet them."

"Just say the word and I will be there," he answered. He kissed her on the cheek, and the bus left him standing among the drunks coming out of the Wellie.

Life went on at the camp and Martin managed to visit Olivia a number of times at her office.

"Why don't you come round tonight, Martin and I will make you supper, and you can meet my housemates?" She smiled as she looked at Martin for an answer.

"I can make it about eight o'clock, but unfortunately I have arranged to go sailing with Geoff de-Kok at four o'clock, and I just cannot let that old bugger down."

"Of course," she smiled, and added, "I will look forward to that."

28

UP HELLY AA

The festival of Up Helly Aa is normally celebrated in mid-winter but because of the long nights in that part of the world it is sometimes held at the end of the season in the main town Lerwick. The darkness at this time of year, with intense cold and wind to match, provides the biggest excuse for the locals to celebrate and have some fun, and this festival gives them just that.

The evening normally starts with the procession of men clad in traditional Viking warrior clothes, complete with a steel helmet, horns and burning torches. False beards are worn and some paint their faces for effect; fur waistcoats and bright red shirts with gold buttons and trimmings replace the normal fur-lined parka coats. The procession looks magnificent – the colour of dress, the happiness of the smile, the animated energy and the sheer enthusiasm of everyone concerned.

At the end of the march, the mass of party revellers, all now worse for drink, convene close to the ship and march around the vessel throwing the torches into it as they pass.

It is the replica of a traditional Viking boat meticulously built by local Shetland craftsmen only to be set alight and destroyed for fun.

As the flames fan the vessel, it starts to disintegrate and the revellers now feel it is time to leave, so together with family and friends they all slowly fade into the night.

With a vast number of the site workers travelling to Lerwick for the festivities, Barney thought it would be a good time to carry out his first real action.

He had talked with members of the social club, obtained from them the transport arrangements for the night and made a note of the bus timetable and location of pick-up points. He had reviewed 'pick-up' and 'drop-off' times for the revellers, and calculated the earliest time the first bus would arrive back at the ship. He then allowed for a safe window that would allow him to carry out what he needed to do, added a contingency, with adequate time left for him to gain a vantage point to watch the fun.

The scheduled time of the last pick-up on the way to Lerwick was 20:20 hours and the first bus to return was scheduled for 02:30 hours from Lerwick. He decided on a four-hour working period starting at 21:00 hours and finishing at 01:00 hours; this would give him ample time to pack up and motor to a suitable place to get a good view of the proceedings.

When visiting the ship previously to have dinner with Martin, and whilst waiting for him in the car park, he noticed that just adjacent to the gangway there was an interesting set-up that would give him the break that he was seeking.

He observed that a ledge on the edge of the quayside ran alongside the whole length of the ship; there was enough space for a man to move along it without danger.

He noticed also, hanging directly under the gangway, what appeared to be a string of. white balls similar to small mooring balls for rowing boats and these were hanging under the whole length of the gangway.

By his calculation, he could pack an adequate charge into

one of the balls that would bring down the entire structure. It would be necessary to ensure there was no one crossing at the time, as at this stage he certainly did not want casualties.

To access one of the balls that would hold the charge, he would need to climb down the side of the quayside, and by edging along the ledge he could then reach it.

With the aid of a rope tied around his waist for safety, he could easily access the ball and either pack the charge there in situ or remove it and do it away from the jetty.

He estimated to use about two kilos of explosive with a primary charge set off by an alarm clock.

The buses were expected back at the ship two hours after midnight. He planned to wind up his work at 01:00 hours which would allow him adequate contingency.

He laughed as he thought about the bad language this would cause, with the ship minus its gangplank and the guys stranded on the quayside. It would totally inconvenience the whole of the ship, and the men stranded onshore in bitterly cold weather full of drink would make the situation tense.

The police would be confused, running around like headless chickens; it would surely be a sight for sore eyes.

Declan would no doubt hear about the incident on the news and would wish he could be at the ship to see the upheaval. Barney intended the action to be a statement of intent and put the whole island in wake-up mode.

It would also make the security nervous of what could be lurking when the site was officially opened but he felt confident that nobody would suspect Declan or himself; they were too popular and friendly with people socially and at work. The most important achievement would be this – the ability to build the charge, manage it, and successfully execute.

His prowess in bomb-making would be proven and he would have the self-esteem that he craved, and the respect from his peers.

At the design and construction management offices, Martin worked his normal week and his friendly attitude made him a hit with the canteen staff, the tea and cleaning ladies. They all usually came and started work in the afternoon to work the evening shift.

One of the ladies was a particularly nice person of about forty, with whom Martin had become quite friendly. They were discussing the forthcoming festival and she was explaining the history and tradition attached to it, and the reasons behind the timing of such an event.

During the conversation she suggested that he accompany her to the festival, as she had two free tickets, and asked Martin to come at the start of the evening to her house where she would introduce him to those involved in arranging the event.

On the Friday, the lady gave Martin the two entry tickets and the place where he would meet her on the day. She was married and her husband was involved in the festival organizing committee and would be busy most of the night. He took the tickets and agreed to pick her up at Lerwick bus terminal.

However, later that night Martin had second thoughts regarding the arrangements and persuaded a friend, Dave Besant, to take the tickets instead and fill in for him for the night with the lady. Dave was enthusiastic – he was already acquainted with the lady in question.

Martin decided to go to the festival anyway, as his friend Geoff had a spare ticket, so later that night he travelled with his friend to Lerwick.

Through the crowd at the festival, Martin saw Dave and the cleaner; they were enjoying themselves, but there was not so much as a nod of acknowledgement from either of them. Martin now felt a party pooper because he had passed on his tickets to Dave with an excuse but still had turned up on the night.

The procession was vibrant with lots of shouting and laughing, but the weather was still cold with rain in the air. It did not stop the festivities and after a long wait the boat was set alight accompanied by loud cheering.

The bus was due at 02:00hrs, but the night was cold and the drink started to wear off, and the night dragged on. Dave Besant finished the night early, feeling that he was out of his depth with the family and friends that he did not know.

It wasn't them as much as his own feeling of being uncomfortable, so he decided to try for an early lift back to the ship.

At the fire, heads began to throb, throats dry and the burning of the boat was now down to its last dying embers. The last of the people standing just gazed as the embers as they blew in the early morning wind.

The redeeming feature for those from the terminal was the large collection of beer still intact on the bus and this would be like gold dust to those waiting to board, their spirits now seriously flagging. Geoff, as usual, was full of spirits and the hour journey back to the accommodation seemed to Martin an eternity.

People with drink have a tendency to think that they are fantastic singers with no shame, hitting flat notes, warbling ridiculously rather than singing, secretly imagining they are performing at the Albert Hall rather than on a bus in the Shetland Islands.

The louder they become the flatter the notes, always under the impression they sound fantastic. Rugby songs do not need to be sung by a Caruso – the louder and cruder they are sung then the better effect that they have on the listeners, most of whom are drunk at this stage anyway.

Martin covered his head, trying desperately to muffle out the noise, and at every chorus when the voices were at their loudest he covered his ears with his hands. He could not wait to get back to the ship and get his head down on the pillow, because a long day of work was ahead of him.

His staff had been reduced recently, with two released for poor performance and had since been replaced with engineers now available from the mainland sites.

However, since his friend Geoff had left for work in the head office he had not been replaced, and the additional work was becoming tiresome.

29

THE MASTER AT WORK

APRIL 1979

Barney waited until the sound of the last bus had departed from the quayside, heading towards the event. It seemed an eternity before the last of the engines faded and the night fell silent; it was the start of his first real action. He carefully collected the secondary charge from the cottage in Brae and loaded it into his old Land Rover. The primary charge and fuse were stowed in his carry bag.

Once at the quayside, he parked and left the vehicle in the bushes. Then he slipped down by the water's edge and manoeuvred his way along the bank until he was almost at the stern of the ship.

There was music coming from the top deck, and he could see the heads of some guys playing pool in the games room. Silently he made his way along the long narrow ledge to the amidships position where the gangplank was in position and carefully reached over and loosened one of the white balls hanging down.

With it safely in his hands he made his way back to the exit point and slowly walked back to his vehicle. Inside the vehicle he cut a small enough hole in the plastic to allow him to position the charge and the detonator, and after checking the device he set the alarm for 01:30 hours.

Checking the device for the last time and holding the ball carefully in the upright position, he returned to the ship. It was still quiet on his return, and he slipped down the side of the quayside and onto the ledge.

Making his way along the side of the ship, he positioned the plastic ball in the place from where he had removed it, and checked it for stability. Happy with the situation, Barney then returned to the vehicle and drove back to the camp.

The waiting was the big thing for Barney, and in trying to keep himself awake he made endless cups of coffee. He checked his watch over and over again, and nervously paced up and down in his room, and though confident everything was correct, he nevertheless felt edgy.

He would wait until about fifteen minutes prior to the coaches' scheduled return and then drive along the road to Firth, the second camp, where he could set up his viewpoint from a safe distance.

At exactly 01:00 hours Barney steered the Land Rover on the road to Brae, but turned off the road about a mile from the entrance to the Firth camp, and stopped when he reached the water's edge. Taking out his binoculars, he focused on the side of the white cruise liner.

At 01:10 hours a taxi pulled up in the ship's car park, and a figure appeared to get out and pay the driver. *Who the bloody hell is that at this time*, thought Barney and looked at his watch; it was now 01:13 hours. Barney delicately adjusted the binoculars and brought the figure into view. The taxi swivelled on the gravel and swung off to the direction of Brae. The figure remained motionless, and his body was in a position to suggest that he was either counting his money or having a pee.

Barney was not sure who it was, but the shape of the guy looked like someone who was on Martin's site. He was not a boxer but Barney knew that they had met and the guy's name was Dave. He became impatient and thought he might have to go quickly and defuse the devise. He checked his watch – 01:21 hours.

"What the bloody hell is Dave doing?" he said to himself, and again focused the glasses.

Dave appeared to be staggering along the gangway, but he was moving slowly and even appeared to stop. Barney checked his watch – it was 01:27 hours.

"No man! No!" squealed Barney. He checked his watch.

At precisely 01:30 hours, looking through the glasses, he scanned to see the position of Dave. It seemed that he had thankfully disappeared, and just in time, for now he was expecting a flash followed by noise… but there was nothing!

He now hoped that the device would not explode at random with people on the gangway and cause fatalities, as that would be disastrous.

He waited.

Nothing happened.

Waiting for a few more minutes with the gangway and surrounding area looking totally deserted, he wondered what his next move would be, and then decided to keep to his original plan and head back to camp.

Now out of his mind with worry he decided the best thing to do was to rest up in his room; he did not want to get caught at the scene if the thing suddenly discharged.

He was nervous and became nearly distraught as he opened his room, and there on the floor was a slip of white paper:

'Returned early. Do not know where you are. Need to speak with you. Love Rose'.

It was Declan, and Barney was in no mood to talk with his friend now so would wait until the morning. He decided to get some sleep and then confront him outside of his housing block at 06:30, in less than five hours' time.

It seemed even colder when he walked from his accommodation block and made his way towards his rendezvous with Declan, the sleep still in his eyes

"Where the fuck were you last night?" hissed Declan.

"I was down at the ship," answered Barney, and added, "I wanted to stamp our presence on the island so attached a small device to the gangplank."

"You did fucking what?" Declan raised his voice, and nearly choked on his words.

"I could not contact you and discuss it, but wanted a trial run, and with the Up Helly festival, thought it was a good chance."

"No, no and no! That will put everyone on edge and every man and his dog will be looking for us. So what happened?"

"Nothing," said Barney and went on to explain.

"Look, find a reason to go to the ship and find out how the land lies, and release that bloody charge from the ball, then phone me with what has transpired since last night, but make your explanation simple and minimal."

Barney drove to the ship with the excuse made with his foreman that he was to pick up Martin and was to take him to work.

As he pulled up on the quay, his face paled as he noticed that the white ball that contained the explosives was no longer in place. He got out of the vehicle and walked towards the gangplank, then stopped, totally transfixed.

Looking down at the water between ship and shore he noticed a white ball bobbing in the waves at the stern of the ship. He saw it just for a second and then the current whisked it around the stern of ship and it disappeared out to sea.

Begorra, he thought, *that could have blown a bloody hole in the bloody hull.*

Trying not to look conspicuous he casually walked to the stern, only to see the white blob in question some fifty yards out to sea and it seemed the current was taking it out fast.

"What the hell are you doing here at this time of the day?"

Barney turned to see Martin at the end of the gangplank.

"Oh I was sent here to pick up a visitor, but it seems that he has not turned up," answered Barney.

"I didn't see any strangers at breakfast, but then I wasn't looking," said Martin.

"OK, I will get to work. See you later," shouted Barney and jumped in the Land Rover.

Declan answered the telephone, as he was waiting for the call. "Well?"

"The boat's out to sea," informed Barney, disguising the meaning.

"Then I suggest you meet it at the next port of call, but do not let it sail away." He put the phone down.

What do I do now? Barney was undecided.

He tried to collect his thoughts: he needed to hire a boat and retrieve the white ball, just in case it was picked up, became unstable and exploded. All balls were still in place along the gangplank with the exception of one, and this was now floating somewhere at sea.

He had the company Land Rover and could not make any excuses if he delayed going to work. And to drive about the countryside during working hours was not an option. He drove back to his site office and decided to address his foreman with an open mind.

"Look, Colin, I need to pick up a parcel from my mum at the Brae post office, and it would be best if I could nip out, and I will be gone for less than an hour." Colin did not answer but continued perusing the drawings on the desk in front of him.

"I will be as quick as I can," Barney added nervously.

"OK, but drive carefully and make sure that you inform your team; it's really them who need to agree, not me."

"Thanks sir, I will make it up to you and will let the team leader know where I have gone."

Barney drove like a madman once he left the gates of the site and headed to Brae, where he intended to hire a boat and look for the white ball. It wasn't easy trying to find a small boat company that had vessels to hire.

Brae was a small village originally inhabited by the ancient Britons, later the Vikings, but the last thousand years had seen little action, other than the local fishermen, and they lived in the crofts around the water's edge.

Then came along the oil industry and most of the youngsters found better and easier ways to make a living. But the local men who were too old to change their ways continued with their life at sea and still continued to bring home the fish.

It was one of these elders whom Barney approached near to his croft and asked if he could suggest where he could hire a boat.

"Now donna rush things too much, young 'un, and sit ye down here beside me and tell me what you are saying." The old man seemed kind and receptive and encouraged Barney to sit down and explain what he wanted. Barney sat down and made up some cock and bull story about the reasons he wanted a boat.

When he left the old man at the small quayside near to his croft he felt like he had been robbed! Although the man was receptive and gentle, nonetheless he had relieved Barney of £100 for an hour's use, and this would double if he did not return by the hour. To make matters worse, when he checked the outboard petrol tank, he found that he needed to pay extra for fuel which the same nice old gentleman filled up for him and took the extra money with a smile.

Barney was cold and wet after an hour skirting the coastline in the small boat, the surf continually spraying up at him when the bow of the boat bounced on the waves.

He never found anything nor did he see anyone for all his hard work.

The water he encountered was very choppy, with visibility down to only about 15 metres and it was almost impossible to navigate.

His troubles increased with the spray, the movement of the boat and the cold. The task to find a small white ball impossible. It was like finding a needle in a haystack.

He was also aware the device could explode at any minute. He felt useless and depressed and could only think of returning safely to the quay and admitting defeat.

Declan was angry when they met later at the normal rendezvous. "Barney, how the fuck did you manage to get us into this mess? First of all making the fucking bomb and then the fucking thing does not work, and then you lose it!"

"I was only trying to stamp our credentials on the camp," stammered Barney.

"Stamping your own credentials, you mean, and why the fuck did you not mention this to me?"

"You were away on the mainland!"

"No more, please do not say anything more, and never ever do this to me again. Because of all this we will make our strike in August this year, so make your plans for the device, and before you start, advise me of the type, the ingredients, the size and the bloody fuse. We will test it up in the bog somewhere a week or so before the date, so I will meet you down at the Brae cottage on 10th June."

"Who will be the target?" asked Barney.

"I don't know as yet but if we cannot find any important people to waste, then we will go for the process plant. The fractionation columns might be our best bet."

He thought for a moment then corrected himself.

"No, Barney, the best plant to hit will be the power station and the turbines or alternators, but whatever is our first hit may be our last because they will not have far to travel to find two stupid fucking Irishmen. And they know one will not be Johnnie Caldwell!"

30

A BLEEP FOR THE FUTURE

AUGUST 1979

Barney and Declan were going through partnership difficulties with the recent debacle causing friction between the two.

"It is the time, Declan; we must do our thing soon, otherwise what are we here for? We must act."

"OK, OK, Barney, calm down. I know we must do something."

Barney went on, "Now is the time to make an impression, as we have been pretending for too long. It must take place during 1980."

"OK, I will see what I can do."

The summer and autumn of 1979 dragged, and the Irishmen continued to work and wait, but they were growing restless and their small cell was ready to go. However, expectation was going to take a dent and it would happen quite unexpectedly at the end of August. Their Irish bosses had not made contact for a few weeks, and after returning from work, Barney jumped from the van and shouted to the men, "See you guys tomorrow." Slowly, he walked up the hill to his accommodation.

He caught up with two of the guys from work who had joined their friend who was coming down the hill and was preparing for the night shift. The friend was twisting his face into a scowl, and the hatred was spilling from his mouth.

"Bastards, I am telling you. That scum should be wiped from the face of the earth."

Barney looked at the man trying to ascertain what his problem was. Bemused, he waited to hear any further outbursts in the hope that he may piece together what the man hated so much. The man was distraught, and looked at his two friends without moving and then turned his gaze to Barney.

"What... what happened?" asked Barney.

His accent could not be disguised and the man turned away as if in disgust.

Barney dropped behind the other three men as they walked up the hill. After a few strides, the man with the scowl suddenly turned on his heel and walked back the way that he had come.

"Sorry about my friend but he feels strongly about the PIRA atrocities."

"Don't worry, I understand," answered Barney but he lied; he wanted to know why the man was so upset.

AN INCIDENT

AUGUST 1979

Barney was hunched in the chair when Declan pushed open the door and slid silently into the room.

"Hi, old boy, what is so important?" he quizzed.

At first Barney did not stir, and continued to stare at the window hardly blinking.

"Come on, my good man, spill the beans; it cannot be that bad," prompted Declan.

"Coming up the hill tonight, I was told that the boys from the South Armagh brigade have done a job on the bloody British army."

"Done a job? What do you mean, a hit?" asked Declan.

"You can say that again, it seems like a bloody massacre, and in two places at the same time," explained Barney. He went on, "In fact it makes me bloody feel sick, the whole thing."

"Calm down, and don't get carried away, these things happen," assured Declan.

Both men were silent for a while, and Barney looked intently at Declan.

"The first I think was the worst, because the brigade took out none other than Earl Mountbatten, you know, the Queen's cousin, war hero and a tired old man, not directly associated with the turmoil we are in."

"Earl Mountbatten!" screeched Declan. "How and where did this happen?" he enquired.

"I don't know too much, but they blew up his boat, with him and some youngsters in it, possibly his grandsons."

"And the second?" queried Declan.

"The second was at least against the army, but the worst yet with nearly twenty killed in two explosions."

"Where?"

"Mountbatten got it near Sligo, and the soldiers in Warrenpoint."

"Warrenpoint?" Declan raised his voice.

"Yes, old friend, right on our own doorstep." Barney shook his head.

"To say the least that is close to home," and Barney said this with disdain.

"Now come on, Barney, you are the man, you just cannot let this faze you now."

"It just makes me sick, with old men and youngsters involved," said Barney.

Neither spoke for a while, engrossed in their own thoughts.

"I will go and we will talk tomorrow, but we are in this, Barney, and you will need to get your head around this situation."

He left as quietly as when he came in, and Barney remained hunched in the chair.

He remained there until very late, and climbed into bed with a troubled mind.

Declan was concerned about Barney, and now needed to bring his bomb-maker to heel, and convince him that it was the norm, the world they lived in, where other people and even children may be hurt, but the struggle will go on.

Declan's head was spinning, but he knew the importance to get Barney back on course.

The following night after returning from work, Declan

armed with newspapers slipped into Barney's room, and found his friend, already poring over the account of the bombings.

Declan waited and without saying a word, sat on the side of the bed.

To make noise for security reasons he turned on the television, and waited for his friend to open the conversation.

"I understand what we put ourselves up for, Declan, but the sheer brutality of this thing leaves me cold." Barney was white and drawn as he turned to his old friend and added, "In two strokes so many people killed and maimed and the youngsters, even the Irish, are blown to smithereens."

"Sure it is bad and shocking but we may be called to do the same, and we must be ready, at all costs, because that is what we are, and it is too late to go back. Mountbatten was seventy-nine and a lady dowager was killed with him."

"What irks me is that a young Irish boatman and a young grandson of Mountbatten also died; what did they know?" queried Barney.

"If that is how you feel, then let's make sure it is only soldiers when we are ready to go." Declan realized the mistake he had made after saying this.

"There are no bloody soldiers here, so what do we do, wait for the Queen to open the terminal and send her after her cousin? Do you think we will feel happy with that?"

Declan also felt negative for the first time and did not have the words to change the way Barney was feeling.

Barney went on quoting from the newspaper. "The first 500 lb fertilizer bomb was hidden in a hay cart and detonated by remote control, killing six soldiers. The Irish by studying the British army tactics knew that the British would set up a command unit in the gatehouse, and set a 800 lb bomb hidden in some milk pallets, that was detonated by remote control a half hour after the first one. This time twelve soldiers were killed, amounting to a total of eighteen."

When Barney had finished, he paused and fell silent for a few moments then added, "The first explosion was so fierce that it burned the British driver's pelvis to the seat he was sitting on. The second explosion blew the officer's head clean off and it was found in the nearby stream. These are the gruesome details that I do not feel comfortable with," said Barney.

He was putting his point across and stated almost as a challenge to Declan.

"We must make a plan, Barney, so finish your bomb and we will discuss our target."

"That sounds good, thanks."

"We can do some mischief to the economy big time here, without the gruesome detail," added Barney and he seemed to have accepted the situation.

Declan left the room without another word, and headed back to his accommodation, leaving Barney still transfixed by the newspaper. Declan walked hurriedly in the cold wind, knowing in his mind that he may need to lead his friend along the dark road gently. Barney would need to dedicate himself totally in preparing the devices that were required. Declan knew in his heart of hearts that he may have to carry out the bombing himself.

It was necessary that he know everything about how Barney worked and keep close to him whilst he did it, for he felt that his old friend would not survive the pressure.

32

A GLITCH IN INTELLIGENCE

SEPTEMBER 1979

The offices were now finished and looked immaculate on the top of the hill overlooking the site. Shaped like an 'E' with each spur occupied by different contractors they shared a bright new reception area.

The hub of the client staff remained in the site offices near to the main gate. These were located about 600 metres from the offices on the hill. Life in all the offices was extremely civil with tea and coffee served at 10:30 and light food available to purchase if required.

Exactly on the dot of 15:30 Dave Osley and Martin left the offices to drive back to the accommodation and carry the collection from the slot machines. It was to be their sixth slot machine coin collection since taking over the duties of social club treasurer; it always crossed their minds why they had let themselves in for such a task.

They had three different locations for collection, each positioned a fair distance from the other and they estimated the time taken would be about fifty minutes. After their first stop, Dave was particularly interested in counting the weekly takings and making a comparison with those taken prior to their time doing the job.

Both Dave and Martin had studied the receipts from the slot

machines over a number of weeks before they started and over the same time after.

Dave concluded the average takings by the previous collectors were £3,200, against the average since they took over for the same time period of £5,215.

"How long and why do you think that this situation prevailed?" asked Martin as Dave splashed through puddles.

"Don't go there." Dave screwed his face. "As long as we are clean, I will be happy."

"Wise words, and you're right, the important thing is that we keep records. With the mood of the punters they will have us all out and off the site."

They carried on with their duties in silence and the first two stops went without event, the centres almost empty and apart from two cleaners they saw no one. The third and final stop was the common room on the edge of the camp. Both were silent as they carried the bags through the swing doors towards the open plan area that adjoined the kitchen.

The gaming machine stood between the kitchen and tables, tactically to attract attention as people passed. Next to the machine was a set of half a dozen stairs that led up to two small conference rooms.

As Dave knelt down to unlock the bottom of the machine allowing the takings to drop, both of them were suddenly aware of talking in the nearest common room.

They glanced at each other, and without saying a word knew what the other was thinking – *not again*.

Dave looked up and with a cold stare held his forefinger to his lips, and they froze, because the conversation in the common room seemed to be getting out of hand.

"They need to make up their fucking minds!" The man's voice was remonstrating with whoever was in the room with him.

"Barney, we know what the task is and that is to play mischief when they open the site in a year's time."

"But what mischief, and how many?"

"I'm telling yer, Barney, it is the main ceremony and whoever opens it gets our load." Declan was adamant.

"But you know how many troops and security will be there, because before it was the Secretary of State for Scotland and now it's the Queen of England herself."

Martin and Dave looked earnestly at each other.

Martin motioned for Dave to pack up and go.

Dave picked up the money that they'd already collected, but as he did so some coins moved inside the bag and made a clinking sound.

The voice in the room suddenly changed tone.

"Who the fuck is there, Barney? I thought that this place was out of bounds during the day."

Declan quickly moved to the door and opened it, and listened intently for a few seconds. He put his hands to his lips to silence anything that Barney might blurt out.

He checked the kitchen and walked to the swing doors at the entrance and all was silent.

"Is anyone there?" Barney called.

"No, nothing," answered a relieved Declan. He looked at his watch and said, "We have extended our time, so let's go back to work. We will talk as we walk."

"Then what have we decided?" Barney was confrontational.

"No change – we make a plan for the first trial, and the location of the devices at the opening."

"But you take notice of what I said," pleaded Barney. "We still want our photographs on the pub wall, don't we, so we have to make our mark at the opening." He seemed positive.

Declan, still conscious of his surroundings added, "Make the test piece and I will order the materials and transport."

"But the best material is gelignite," urged Barney. "Most of the smart commanders use it, and it's reliable."

"No, it will be ammonia nitrate as the tertiary charge, with both a detonator and a booster." Declan was being assertive.

"I remember that at training school we demonstrated that about 6g of (DDNP) diazodinitrophenol was utilized as the primary. It is non-toxic, easy to make and not sensitive." He now started to boast. "I learnt that DDNP is fairly stable when storing, and will not detonate if unconfined." He went on showing his knowledge. "It should be stored moist but must be dried before packing." Barney felt better he had got that off his chest.

He kept up his conversation on their way to the car park, but now outside, Declan interrupted his friend, unemotional in what his friend had been talking about.

"I will meet you on the mainland at the normal place and we will do the two test pieces," his words decisive.

"OK," said Barney, "I will be ready."

At the car park, Declan stopped and stared at the old Land Rover parked next to theirs.

"Whose vehicle is that?" he nodded towards the Land Rover.

"Strange," answered Barney, "I am sure it was not there when I came."

"OK, we must not linger, let's go."

They were both in good spirits as they drove back to the site, and forgot the incident regarding the Land Rover.

Barney was due on leave the next day, three days ahead of Declan, and intended to enjoy himself before meeting with his friend in Cumbria in three days' time.

Martin and Dave were shocked regarding their recent experience, even though both had not heard the whole dialogue between the Irishmen but they had heard enough to make them both very wary.

"What do we do now?" asked a shocked Dave Osley.

Martin was wide-eyed. "It was the lad Barney. He is the kid who has been to the gym these last few weeks."

"Look," said Dave, "we cannot say anything about this at the moment."

"Why not?"

"Because the bloody Irish may kill us." He looked perplexed then added, "And if we tell anybody, they probably wouldn't believe us."

They drove back to the office slowly and in silence, both collecting their thoughts.

33

A BIT OF A WHOOSH

SPRING 1980

It was early in April when Barney took the train down to the border between England and Scotland. He disembarked at Lancaster and transferred to a small diesel-electric train that took him to Cartmel, a small village famous for its National Hunt racing.

It was a short walk to the farm where they had rented two cottages and these were about a mile away from the main farmhouse. They were basically two up and two down and at the back of the houses were an array of outhouses positioned 30 metres from the cottages. These were used previously as workshops but were now in a state of disrepair and dilapidated. Barney unpacked the material that he had collected at the station and laid it out on the floor of the cottage and feeling tired, retired to bed where he slept soundly.

Early the next morning he laid out the fertilizer ANNM and this he checked contained at least 30% nitrogen, the exact amount that he had requisitioned from the stores.

Barney decided to detonate using a primary booster, although as this was to be a simulation of the real thing, he used a ratio of the quantities that he was to use on the day.

Re-examining the plans that he had made up on site, he

measured out the quantities carefully. His main charge was 15 kg, his secondary charge about 1 kg with a primary of 1 g. The electrical circuit that would detonate the primary device was wired up to a signal from a cheap alarm clock.

He had two days to prepare the device and hoped that his ingenuity this time would surprise and please Declan when he arrived. His preparation looked good to him, and he was content with his general inventiveness. This was adding to his know-how .

The following day, the charges would be ready and he would start to confine them into their packages, leaving the electrical signal device – an alarm clock – to the last.

Now brimming with confidence regarding his day's work he retired to bed early, fully intending to connect the wiring in the morning prior to Declan arriving.

THE FOLLOWING MORNING

It had rained the night before and Barney confined the charges for all three devices. He then placed the contraption in the outhouse, less the wiring. As he left the building, and for security, he shut the old oak door and its rusty hinges creaked as he latched it in place.

As he entered the downstairs living room to boil the kettle, he was momently stopped in his tracks by a loud bang, followed by three similar retorts. Now totally alarmed and quite deaf from the noise he became disorientated.

The pattern of the bangs continued for a few minutes, and holding his ears, he quickly moved to the window to see what was happening. Just outside, not more than twenty yards away, he saw two young men apparently shooting at rabbits, using shotguns.

In complete panic he dashed out of the cottage to confront

them, his intention being to persuade them to move on as quickly as possible in case they discovered his device in the outhouse.

As he ran to plead with the men, who were between him and the outhouse, one of them took a step forward, aimed, and discharged one barrel at a target in the direction of the outhouse.

In one blinding second, a massive explosion broke the serenity of the area and both men had their hats blown high into the air, debris rained down on the onlookers who were now flat on the floor, mud covering faces and clothes.

Slate and glass pieces fell for many minutes about them, the remnants strewn all around, dropping from the sky like rain and the men on the ground covered their heads with their hands for whatever protection they could muster. All three remained inert on the ground for many minutes, each expecting the second phase.

"Jesus, Mary and Joseph, what in God's name was that?" exclaimed Barney.

The men slowly walked to the point of the explosion with Barney carefully tracking them from behind.

"Is there gas in those outbuildings, Jake?" one of the men asked.

"Not as I know, Ben. That was disconnected years ago as far as I know," answered his friend.

"Then let's tell the farmer when he gets back and explain what has happened. Perhaps he can tell us."

"Not much left of that door, or the building for that matter," cried Jake.

"It needed a clear out, and it will save us doing it." Ben seemed relieved now that he was over the shock.

"You all right, mate?" asked Jake looking at a shocked Barney.

"Yes, fine," stammered Barney.

And the two men walked slowly away as if nothing had happened.

"Whatever you got in that there gun, then I want some of it, mate," joked Jake and with that, they strolled away as cool as you like.

ONE HOUR LATER

"What the fuck happened here?" Declan was absolutely astounded at the mess around the cottage. Tiles, rock and debris covered the ground and the outhouse now looked how London must have looked after the Luftwaffe onslaught in 1940. "Begorra, I have never seen the like of this mess ever." Declan was amazed. "It looks like a bloody bomb has hit it." Declan stared at the ruins of the small house.

Slowly and deliberately he turned his head towards Barney. "Is this anything to do with you?" He glared at the man.

"I meant is as a surprise, really. I had worked on this for months and it would have been a wonderful surprise for you if those two idiots had not arrived with their bloody shotguns."

"It is a surprise, you fucking nutter! Do you know that about 30% of accidents in the US are related to explosions carried out by untrained people?" He was aghast! "And another point, my fine friend, did you know Che Guevara, the terrorist and mass murderer, sent his men to manufacture and build explosives, and for the record at least half of them blew themselves up as a consequence? And you know why this was? It was because they did not follow instructions or were not aware of the safety codes for making explosives." He was almost breathless. "Barney, my friend, I have told you before and I reiterate it now, never, never, ever do this thing again without talking with me about it first." He paused then added, "I suppose that we need to disappear from this place tonight, otherwise there may be questions that we cannot answer when the police arrive."

That night they checked in at a local hotel, ready for an early start in the morning.

It was cold on the platform at Carnforth as they awaited the 06:30 train from Barrow-in-Furness to Lancaster.

Declan looked cold and unshaven, and glanced at Barney who was trying to sleep.

"Barney, pay attention, man, we need to go over this situation again to understand what was good about it and what was not!"

"What is it we need to discuss, Declan? I am not in the bloody mood. I spent three days preparing the device, all but the primary, and left it in the outhouse for safety until you arrived before detonation, but what am I expected to do about people with guns?"

"Firstly, the bomb went off without, you say, a remote detonator."

"Yes, but as I told you it was that fool of a man who fired his gun at the shed."

"But was the device detonated by shock, by vibration or by heat?"

"How the bloody hell do I know. It just went off, didn't it?"

"OK but the mixture of material; tell me more, but before you do let me tell you how lucky you were."

And Barney explained the whole procedure from ordering the material to confining the charges.

In the end Declan said, "OK, Barney, let's start making the next charge and this time it will be carried out under the earth and we will detonate remotely, and I will be there to supervise, understand?"

34

A GOOD REASON FOR AN EXCUSE

MAY 1980

Martin was busy helping Barry to set up the new boxing gym in the Northern Centre on the first floor. It was looking good with all the bags and bench apparatus in position and now with Robby's expertize the team was seeing the best way to fix a pad over the corner ropes, and cover any hard spots on the corner post.

Robby had been involved in this type of problem with boxing rings for all of his life, and his old manager, Tommy Gilmour, had taught him all that he knew. The idea was to hang the pad from the top of the post over the top of the ropes all the way down to the bottom of the post and clip both ends. This way a soft pad would reduce any impact to the boxer if he was trapped on the ropes and his head was forced over the top of the post.

Robby's designs usually worked well but were always over-elaborate with more than enough bits and pieces, but the team had little choice but to bow to superior knowledge.

However, this time his mind worked a little more simply than usual, and his proposal seemed quite adequate. A local fabricator was contacted and he advised how his simple clips and clasps design would work, Martin advised him the sketches would be forwarded, and the price was then confirmed.

"Yer know, Martin, a boxer can lean back against the corner and if his head stretches onto the post the injury can be fatal."

"Good on yer, Robby, you're the man."

Robby grinned and seeing a familiar face who was skipping in the corner said, "You see, laddie, that the Irishman has returned," and nodded towards a man skipping.

Barney had been spending more sociable time at the gym, as he found the challenge of sparring and training a great relaxation. The boxing trainers on duty at the time always paired up the boxers and ensured that the two were almost the same standard.

Barney was here for a reason other than keeping fit and was listening and taking note as he watched the time on the overhead clock. During one of his visits to the gym he had overheard Martin and Robby discussing the ring post protection idea and offered to do any errands that were necessary.

It was especially attractive to Barney because he had overheard that the fabricator had his workshops in Brae and this would be a great opportunity to visit the cottage.

It could also give him an alibi if spotted in the area, plus it gave him access to his workshop. He had been especially busy in recent weeks and had managed to collect a lot of raw material that he had stored in the garage of the cottage. The material was mostly ammonium nitrate that was normally sent in parcels through the post.

He had also received a plastic bomb-making substance called Semtex but with only one delivery and little knowledge of assembly he was nervous and left this package alone. The problem was safe storage, and it was important that each of the different material types were kept apart and stored at the right temperature and humidity.

He finished his skipping and taking a few minutes' break he wandered over to Martin and Robby.

"Hi, big fella, please do not forget my offer of running some errands for you guys, as I can get time off to do them and have the wheels."

"Yes, I do remember your offer," replied Robby.

"I can collect the articles from Brae, and deliver them to the gym; it would be no trouble, to be sure," suggested Barney.

Robby smiled. "Thanks, Irish, but we can manage."

Robby felt that Barney should be doing other things, like work, rather than making offers to run errands that were none of his business.

A week later Barney had made a visit to the cottage to make safe some fertilizer that he had left on the garage workbench. To do so he had lied to his foreman regarding time off site and what happened to him next turned out to be a serious problem.

On his way to Brae, Barney was stopped in his car, and charged for speeding by the police. It was a stupid mistake, and basically down to lack of concentration and this would mean further problems with Declan. He needed a good alibi to support his explanation to his employers regarding his presence in Brae and what better than carrying out errands on behalf of the boxing club.

His company would require him to submit an incident form and pay the fine now.

He thought that it was better to explain to his foreman immediately, rather than later if and when the police were called in.

He reported the incident both in a written report and verbally, and in both cases gave an explanation in helping the social club by running an errand. However, what he did not know was that Robby had changed the design and had not sent the sketches into the Brae works at the time the police stopped Barney.

The company transport officer wanted clarification of Barney's story and needed a representative of the social club to verify it. The procedure that Barney had carried out was in order, as he had asked permission from his foreman to leave site in the company Land Rover to carry out this errand for the social club.

Most of the companies on the site supported any social club activities, especially the boxing club, as many of their employees had an interest in the club, and they themselves wanted to maintain good public relations with their men.

It was going to be the responsibility of either Robby or Martin to verify his story, as they were the two who were present when Barney claimed he was asked to do the job. Barney was concerned that such a small incident was causing so much controversy, but the one thing that worried him was his explanation regarding his reasons for being in the village at the time.

He tried to cover all angles but in doing so intended to keep Declan in the loop, so once he arrived back in his office he picked up the phone.

"I have had a problem, a small one that will be resolved quickly I hope."

"What problem?" replied Declan raising his voice. He was now irritated.

"It's just that I have been done for speeding and the company wants someone to vouch for my presence in Brae."

"Have you got someone?" Declan was becoming extremely agitated over Barney's activities in recent weeks and this was just another reason for him to caution him on behalf of the army.

"Yeah, I think so, because the boxing club will do this for me; they are all good mates."

"They had better be, and I think that we need a serious chat, Barney, and soon." There was a pause; Declan added in a disappointed voice, "We will talk tomorrow."

The phone went dead. Declan pondered on the situation.

The target and the date for the opening by the Queen was confirmed in the local paper, but things were not looking good for Barney.

He wanted at least two devices to be prepared and ready at any one time but to complete just one was becoming a challenge. The army had spent time and money on educating Barney on the use and execution of IEDs (Improvised Explosive Devices).

Barney had not been successful in building and initiating these devices, and headquarters was slowly losing confidence in its star pupil.

However, what knowledge he did have was not shared with Declan and the two not working together was of serious concern. Declan decided to start an inventory regarding the materials required to make a device and he would then decide how things would go from there.

Martin made a call to London; the phone rang three times. "George?"

"Yes, who is it?"

"It's Martin. I may have a problem."

"That's interesting; tell me about it," asked George.

"I have a friend, an Irishman who I think is plotting against the Queen," informed Martin.

"That's a big claim, my friend. Have you anything supporting this?"

"Two conversations and the second was confirmed as the person that I have identified," confirmed Martin.

"Is this super urgent or have we time to investigate further?" asked George.

"We have time, and if you want to check the man's name it is Barney Coughlin."

"Thank you. Because of the obvious importance, I will check at once and keep you informed. Keep in touch."

The line went dead, and Martin sat down to give the matter further thought.

35

SPRING SURPRISE

Martin returned from his leave late in May 1980. Spring was always an exciting time of year and he was in good spirits. He was looking forward to his tour of duty. He jumped from the people carrier shuttle bus at the bottom of the hill and made his way slowly upwards dragging his wheelie hand case behind him.

He had relocated his accommodation from the ship to the management block X in the Toft accommodation area as this was the management section of the camp, and it had better access to the gym than the ship, whose exercise facilities were more suitable to an ageing clientele, with wicker chairs and carpets, not a boxing gym.

The accommodation was more spacious with an extra room and a study area attached to the sitting room.

He had moved from the *Stena Baltica* but the ship had left him with some very pleasant memories, and he would certainly miss the comfort that the ship had to offer.

The mess area and the relaxing facilities were second to none, but he felt that with all the pluses of living on a cruise liner, there were better ones in living on a management block on site.

The *Stena*, because of its luxury and reception facilities, was a great hit for any VIPs or celebrities visiting the site. It was very pleasant to walk on the decks before a meal, with a martini in one's hand. Then after the meal, sit in the spacious armchairs in the ship's lounge and discuss the topics in hand, or play a game of pool or bridge in the ship's games room.

Martin had at times assisted the social club events secretary and arranged the visits of entertainment at the camp. The budgets for entertainment were generous and to keep the 'troops' happy, many well-known celebrities appeared at the camp, and where better to house them than aboard the ship, depending on availability of the accommodation suites at the time.

The social committee had arranged the visit of Acker Bilk and his Paramount Jazz Band. Acker and his team stayed in the camp but visited the ship for a late lunch, and then travelled back to Toft for the evening performance.

The show was one that the majority of the camp had waited for but the way it would turn out did not make everyone happy. Acker was famous for his single release, 'Stranger on the Shore', and it was the longest single record that held top spot in the charts.

The Northern Centre on the night was above capacity with people standing in the most testing of places, just to get a good view of proceedings. His show went well throughout until his most famous number started. A few minutes after the start a worker together with his home-made clarinet crawled up on stage and joined in with Acker. No sooner had this started, than the hall fire alarm was set off and drowned everything else in the hall. The noise of the alarm, the monotone background noise of the improviser and Acker continued through to the end.

The only thing that was bigger than this rude interjection was the unperturbed and professionalism of the entertainer himself, who carried on as if nothing was happening.

Martin's mind was on these memories as he continued his trudge up the hill, and was brought out of his dream by a greeting by his old mate Dave Osley.

"Hi mate," said Dave sullenly.

"What's up?" exclaimed Martin rather surprised that Dave was sober this Saturday afternoon.

"The bastards have done it, mate."

"Done what, Dave?"

"They have done it behind your back while you were on leave; do you know what I mean?" said David.

Martin suddenly became serious, as Dave's words were striking home.

"Tell me about it, Dave, because it sounds that my time is up."

"Nigel, the new construction manager, has done it and is bringing in his own man!"

"Who is that?" Martin asked.

"Don't know but probably a real wanker." Dave was trying to support his friend.

However, Martin was feeling sick, totally empty and felt that it would be best if the earth opened up and swallowed him. He would now have to go to the office, knowing that everyone was aware that he was being given the push. They would almost all say how they felt sorry for him.

"When did this news come out, Dave?"

"The day after you went on leave. Anyway, Martin, I understand that they have options, if that softens the blow."

"What options, Dave?"

"I think the obvious one is to go and take over in Zambia from your old mate de-Kok."

"Yes, I had heard that Geoff had taken that position, apparently filling in for someone like me." Martin just thinking about de Kok made him smile.

"And the other?" Martin was now inquisitive.

"In fact there are two more that you may consider, if you so want," advised Dave. "The first is that you stay here as deputy to the new guy, but I feel that you won't accept a role working for someone else, especially after all the work that you have put in," sighed Dave.

"And the third option?" asked Martin.

"Well the third is a duration for the company down at Bacton-on-Sea on the east coast installing a new process plant and pipeline."

"Do you fancy a drink?" asked Martin.

"No, mate, I have things to do and only did this to give you some warning before you got into the office. But thanks and I will see you around tomorrow." Dave turned and started to walk to his own accommodation block.

On Monday morning Martin got the worst over and put on a brave face for all the management. After a week to take stock of all the pros and cons, he decided that the faster he got away would be for the best.

He had thought closely about the three options.

The first was to stay here and he knew that this was not even a starter.

The second, working down the east coast, certainly did not impress him, and the thought of cold grey mornings starting work on a dirty site made him nauseous.

However, the thought of working in the heart of Africa with the sun and the happy faces around him certainly did.

One of the site's construction superintendents had worked in Kitwe on a previous job and had kept Martin informed of what to expect. He had recommended Zambia and had told his friend of the sun and the happy people, and he said that the flowers were as big as an elephant's head. He went on to inform Martin that the golf courses were top class and the young, local people were mad keen on boxing.

Apart from the challenge of working in difficult conditions assisting in building a cobalt plant, the strength of potential world-class boxers did, and whether the locals were good enough to be international fighters remained to be seen.

After some serious thought it was a no-brainer and he sent an urgent letter to Human Resources accepting the post in Africa.

His first priority before packing his bag and booking a seat on the budgie, was to ring George Webster. The telephone rang a couple of times and Martin did not waste time with niceties.

"Hi George, Martin."

"Yes, old mate, what have you for me?"

"Bad news, George. I have been replaced on site and been transferred to Zambia."

"That is not so good, Martin. What brought this about?"

"Personalities, or something like that," Martin advised.

"Look, Martin, with regards to Coughlin, I checked him out and he is clean. I am not sure where we go with him now."

"He is the man, I assure you, but you may need to act on what I have given you. It is out of my hands now."

"We cannot do anything without sound evidence. Martin, we need you. Do you want me to pull some strings?"

"No, what is done is done. I cannot help you more on this."

"OK, Martin, you have done a great job and kept the flag flying. I will think of something, but in the meantime, let me know when you settle in Africa."

"Thanks George, I will."

He gently put the phone on its rest, and felt a little guilty that he could not help more.

36

BACK-UP PLAN

JULY 1980

"Have you sorted this bloody thing out yet?" Declan was not trying to raise his voice but he was slowly losing patience with his old friend and he held the telephone away from his ear.

"Don't worry, my man." Barney was full of bravado.

"Don't worry, you say, but I am worrying. We are getting close to the important date and things are not yet ready, and the main man is away with the bloody fairies." Declan had lost it.

"He is not away with the fairies and the reason that things are not cleared up is that Martin bloody Valeron has gone for good, and he did so before he was asked a thing about my participation in collecting the items from Brae."

"And the other man on this, this boxing sub-committee?"

"He has gone too, on leave and is taking some holiday also, and will not be back on site for five bloody weeks," sneered Barney.

"OK, if it's gone, it's gone, but never let this happen again, and I repeat, never again."

Barney was quiet, so Declan spoke again, "Then let's get a move on. When do you think that the device will be ready with all associated equipment?"

"Two weeks," answered Barney.

"OK, then we will assess the situation in two weeks."

Declan thought for a moment and then asked Barney, "Where is all this going to be done?"

"I have a place but that is no concern of yours," added Barney cheekily.

"That sort of attitude is not required, Barney, you know whom our allegiance is to, and may I remind you that we have sworn to uphold our promises to the cause; is that how you understand it? And if you do not you will need to let me know. May I remind you, I am the leader of our little pack."

"OK, OK, keep your hair on, I will see you in just over two weeks with my side of the job done." Barney went on, "So you can tell our little tinkers that Barney is on target."

"See you then."

The phone went dead.

Declan was worried that Barney might be getting careless, and he was additionally concerned where Barney was building the device. If it were somewhere that was easily detectable, then the whole plan that they had worked for so long on would be blown.

The situation with Barney was also worrying as the man seemed to have no loyalty for the cause and the whole concept that they were supposed to be living for. He decided not to put too much pressure on his old friend as this might also blow him off track.

GONE AS IF WITH THE WIND

The drone of the HS 747 propeller engines seemed louder than normal and Barney kept his head towards the airplane's porthole, lest someone would recognize him, and his movements may be reported back to administration even before he could clear the country. He began to feel drowsy, and sliding into a snooze, started to dream about his next move. The site would find out that he had left for good and all hell would let loose, he thought to himself. A chase would follow, and this would be from more than a single agency. Barney knew above anything else that he was a hunted man, and he needed to close his tracks wherever he went.

The PIRA, English police, RUC, MI5 and MI6 would all be in the hunt so a change of identification would be the first thing on his agenda. It would be crucial to move fast after disembarkation at Glasgow and he hoped that he could be clear of the UK before this thing became common news. His sudden exit from the Shetland Islands, he thought, may give him at least two days before his departure became known, but time was not on his side.

He body felt numb, his mind blank and empty, he had done all the soul searching, all the 'what ifs' but he had made his decision. He now knew that instead of his photograph hanging in the village pub in glory, his name would be linked as the biggest traitor in Irish history.

He could no longer return home, visit his friends and relatives, visit the local pub or make the trek up to Cloughmore Stone with Declan.

His decision was made based on humanity, the thought of the Englishmen blown to smithereens, their butts burnt onto the armoured car seat, or their decapitated heads found in a stream yards away from the actual blast. All of it sickened Barney through to the core; he was not the man that he'd thought himself to be.

His dreams turned into nightmares when he thought of the child killed with Mountbatten on that dreadful day in August 1979. The cause that he was being trained for was one thing but the unnecessary killing of innocent people, including children, was another and not acceptable in his mind.

He knew that his time now would be lonely, he was on his own, had no history that he could speak of, and may never ever return to his homeland, his beloved Ireland.

Carefully he had planned his escape and intended to disappear as soon as the budgie landed in Glasgow.

He had saved enough money from the rich earnings that he had received on site and he would travel as far as needed, to any continent, to any place that he could find peace away from killing. His family may never ever see him again; the thought was inconceivable but he had done what he had done and there was no going back. A new life in a new country was about to start, and the sooner he could get away the better.

His only regret was upsetting his oldest friend Declan, and he knew he was about to lose him forever.

He arrived at Glasgow airport, disembarked and took a taxi to Glasgow Central railway station, paid the driver, and disappeared into a throng of bustling people.

37

A LONG TWO WEEKS

JULY 1980

Two weeks had passed and not a minute in Declan's life at that time was calm. Every minute, every phone call, he was on edge; he now knew how much he relied on Barney.

Over the last few months Barney had become a touch careless, preoccupied and secretive, but he was his closest friend no matter what the differences now.

Declan asked himself why Barney had left just when they were in sight of launching not only their first attack against the enemy, but the biggest that the world could offer. It was an incredible chance to make a name for themselves and Barney had walked away.

The Queen of England was to open the terminal shortly and the army were expecting big things from him, the headlines would be awesome, the PIRA proud of him!

At first Declan could not accept that Barney had gone, and continued to try and contact him in the normal way. There was no answer on his telephone the first three attempts, and on the fourth time a gruff voice answered, "Yes."

"Sorry to bother you but is Barney Coughlin available?"

"No mate, sorry but he has left. Is there anyone else that you want to speak with?"

"Eh no, thank you."

The phone went dead, and Declan then knew that his biggest nightmare was born into reality… Barney had thrown in the towel.

That evening he went to Barney's accommodation and a new worker occupied it, but he knocked and a bright-faced man of about twenty-three answered the door.

"Sorry, but I thought that my friend Barney Coughlin occupied this room." Declan already knew the answer.

"Sorry mate, I have just started and this is my first night here."

"So you did not know him, I suppose?"

"No mate, I don't know anyone in the camp at the moment, sorry."

"OK thanks," said Declan.

He then went to their normal meeting place to see if there were any messages left by his friend but he found nothing. In despair he made a series of phone calls leaving a code word that would initiate a response.

He then went back to his room to file his report on the current situation, and then more importantly to concentrate and plan an attack that would be more audacious than any in the history of the United Kingdom.

AUGUST 1980
A SECOND PLAN

It had been nearly two months since Barney had absconded from his post in the Shetland Islands. The Republican Army would have serious concerns with Barney should he turn to the police with information regarding the IRA, the strategy and the plans for the May attack on the Queen.

They were not sure of his mental state and continued to

watch his home and previous haunts, as they had serious concerns if he turned his knowledge in to the police.

The intelligence section of the IRA urgently pursued Barney's whereabouts in an effort to guarantee his silence, but because of the secrecy surrounding his work, it was difficult for them to gain the confidence of people without raising suspicions.

On his next R&R Declan left the site, and made his way to the small terraced cottage that they had rented in the Lake District in the north-west of England, different than what they had rented previously.

The cottage this time was near to Newby Bridge on the south side of Lake Windermere.

He arrived at Lancaster station and crossed over to the platform where the small diesel-powered train was waiting, and checked its destination was Barrow and that it stopped at Grange-over-Sands.

He noticed a very frail old lady struggling with her suitcase and took it from her and placed it in the luggage compartment. He turned away and filed into the train where he found two empty seats near a window.

He sat down and slid across to the window seat, but after settling in and feeling comfortable, he suddenly felt a presence beside him.

"Declan, my old friend, how the devil are you?"

Declan looked up and did not recognize his new travelling partner.

"Hello, how are you?"

"Oh, I am great," the man answered.

The eyes met and held contact for a few moments,

"Are you travelling to Carnforth or Grange?" the man asked.

"Grange," answered Declan.

"OK, then perhaps we can walk up to Ma's together instead

of a taxi, and we can discuss Ma and the family and find out how the devil she is," the man queried.

It seemed to the rest of the people on the train that the two Irishmen were travelling home to visit their mammy. They got off the train at Grange-over-Sands and walked through the station gate and out to the road, presenting their tickets to the porter on duty.

Turning left outside the station, they kept in tandem without saying a word. Declan knew that he was held for questioning, simply by the code words expressed by his partner, and felt nervous of the outcome. The man turned slightly to his right and a car that was idling behind them suddenly stopped, the back door opening.

The driver looked straight at the road ahead, whilst the man beckoned Declan to get into the car. It accelerated and drove for about a mile and a half before stopping outside a cottage.

"We will talk inside the house," said the man, then speaking to the driver said, "I will be one hour, please wait." The driver nodded and he turned the engine off.

"My name is McGirk and I am the commander of the Armagh division of the Irish Republican Army."

He did not wait for a response from Declan but moved to the point quickly.

"So, we have two problems to resolve and we need to sort these out quickly. The first is to find our friend Mr Coughlin and let's say curb his responsibilities quickly."

McGirk remained sullen, and he thought before proceeding. "The other is to make our plan and get the materials that we are to use for the opening ceremony."

"OK, Mr McGirk, I have made a plan and drawn out proposals for the IED but I need help to execute the whole thing," explained Declan.

"I am coming to that, my friend. What do you know about the construction of the device we need?"

"Not too much as this was Barney's area. I did the reconnaissance and general planning of the job. With security now being stepped up because of the army's activities, I also need to spend time finding where and when to place the devices."

"You may need now to get involved in both, but I will arrange for a good explosives man to visit you and assist you in this area. The man I am talking about is the best we have, with plenty of experience. Take notice of what he has got to offer and you will benefit immensely. Unfortunately he is working with other divisions at present, and will transfer as soon as possible. What you will not know is that this thing that we are setting up is top priority and to make things more complicated it is being, let's say, sponsored by a third party."

"Who is the third party?" asked Declan.

"It is best that you do not know at this stage, but you will find out in due course." McGirk was not to be drawn.

"Please send your reports promptly and keep the notes to a minimum; always concentrate on important facts." McGirk paused. "Provide me with the location of the blasts and what you require regarding materials. Because of the involvement of others it will be necessary for a bigger team to be involved in your work, so expect interference from time to time, it is that important. Have you any questions?"

Declan didn't ask any.

McGirk continued, "Find out where and when the visitors will be on the day – precisely – and select a position for the blast or blasts."

The discussion abruptly stopped and a short silence followed.

"Please enjoy your leave but we expect you to deliver, my boy! On your next leave you will be contacted in much the same way as this time, but prepare your house for a visitor to stay the whole week, because you will need that time."

Just before he departed McGirk added, "Just send me the details when you have completed them, and keep in touch."

At the end of his rest period, Declan made a booking for the cottage during his next rest period prior to returning to Glasgow.

38

TIME FOR LEARNING

Declan was exhausted, what with the strain of Barney's disappearance and now the extra responsibility from McGirk. It all gave him serious stress and he became extremely depressed and unmotivated. He counted the hours to his next rest period and realized he had never felt so low before. Instead of resting, his days became longer, life faster, most of his days taken up planning the detail of the big day.

Following his flight from Shetland, he took a taxi to Glasgow Central railway station and made his way down to Lancaster. At Lancaster he transferred to the Barrow-bound train and was soon arriving at Grange-over-Sands. It was to be his first real lesson in the build methods of an IED, and he was feeling apprehensive.

He was annoyed with himself that he had missed the majority of lessons when they were held in Dublin, initially set up in the early days, which Barney had attended. The pressure was on him, and he needed to ascertain how and what was needed to make this operation a success.

Billy Keogh was waiting on the platform at Grange, but as the train pulled into the platform, he held back until he had identified Declan. After Declan had disembarked, he sidled up to him and made his introduction.

"I thought that it was Lancaster you were supposed to meet me," said Declan, slightly annoyed that he nearly missed his connection due to looking for the man.

"I taut I had missed you, Declan, so I made my way here instead, but still could not find your bloody house."

Declan, wanting to make headway without any tension between the two, quickly defused the situation. "It's not a problem. Let's get home, have something to eat and you can give me some tips."

"It will need to be more than tips," advised Billy. "Because your life may depend on what I have to tell you," he added.

They ate in silence, a simple pasta dish with a creamy sauce.

Keogh said, "A pint of Guinness would have been nice, but let's have that later; you can buy!"

"There are some simple things that I have heard and do not understand," enquired Declan.

"What are they?"

"What actually is dynamite made up from?"

"Dynamite is made by soaking nitro-glycerine in nitric acid with glycerine. It has been well tried over the years, but we will not be using this method. You should remember, Declan, that most IEDs are made from a nitric acid base, but dynamite is classed as a chemical explosive, and burns rapidly, producing a high gas volume which expands producing extremely high pressure."

"And fuller's earth, what's that? I have heard this term a few times."

"That is the plaster that binds the device together."

Billy suddenly became agitated and said, "We cover most of these in the next few days so don't be concerned."

"It's just that if I do not ask you now, I may forget later and there will still be doubt in my mind."

"OK then, let's clear your head from any other doubts; what's next?"

"What will be the basic composites of the device that we will build?" asked Declan.

"Have not made my mind up yet, but I think it will be a mixture of ammonia nitrate 70%, sodium nitrate 20%, and nitrated resin. AN is the explosive, SN the stablyser with NR helps it to ignite. We will also need a fuse and ignition and this will be discussed in detail sometime over the next few days."

"Why weedkiller and not Semtex or other plastics types that I have heard are more modern and used a lot in the Middle East?"

"The main bulk of the component will be sent through the post shortly before the date, and is virtually harmless in this state; the main thing is, it is unlikely to be detected in the post. We will send the detonator and the primary fuse to you in due course. I take it that we have nowhere to assemble this thing on the island?"

"No," answered Declan, "not since Barney blew our hideout. It took me a week to creep into the cottage and clear up the mess that Barney had left."

They both fell silent.

"Has the army heard anything?" asked Declan.

"Nothing, and we were hoping that you could tell us something."

"Nothing."

"OK, let me brief you on the basics, some you may know."

The explosives expert was completely professional starting with the basic principles and providing Declan with the insights into preparing an IED.

"Remember," went on Billy, "the first thing that is absolutely necessary is a power supply and you cannot do much without that. Usually this is in the form of car batteries, or alkaline flashlight batteries. We need to keep the device as light in weight as possible, for mobility, so the alkaline batteries will be better in this case."

He continued, "The second thing that is required is a switch or activator that will trigger the blast. We will be restricted by time, so it may be best to use a direct firing button, set off by someone in the vicinity. This is an option at present." He paused and as an afterthought said, "Otherwise we can utilize an alarm clock mechanism. There are various other types of switches including radio signal, or other various timers that we can use, including a garage door opener, but realistically it is the alarm clock or direct firing button. The best in my opinion is the direct firing button; it is the most reliable and does not take too much time to set up. The next and most important thing is the big daddy, the main charge, the one that will cause damage, and when it goes it will create history!"

"How big do we want the device?" asked Declan.

"The size of the first bomb used at Warrenpoint was about 220 kg and the second was 360 kg. Both bombs at Narrow Water Castle were planted in static places such as an old building and a stationary truck. The whole operation was carefully planned. We will not have the luxury of a heavy device on the day, as security will be much tighter and the devices need to be easily hidden, light for mobility and fit into a backpack. In my opinion I am suggesting that we plant a series of bombs, set with timers to go off at various intervals. The minor bombs will be excellent decoys; they will cause confusion and the distraction that we will need to set off the main device." He went on, "Perhaps we can build five devices at about 30 kg each."

Declan asked, "Do you have any suggestions how to plant the devices without being detected?"

"Sorry, I am just an explosives man, and it will be up to you to find a way to get in there."

The first lesson went on into the night and the next night,

and on the last three nights Billy Keogh showed Declan the practical way using dummy components.

The following weekend Billy Keogh slipped off into the night, travelled to Sumburgh and the next morning flew back to Glasgow, then onto London and then zigzagged his way quietly to Dublin.

Declan had an intense week, and he was not sure that the notes he had taken would see him through. He would need a trial build, and try not to blow himself up whilst doing it!

39

THE DARK SIDE OF EUROPE

FEBRUARY 1981

The opening ceremony at Sullom Voe was finally confirmed as the spring of 1981, the opening date actually set for 9th May, coinciding with the Queen's state visit to Norway.

Progress at the terminal was behind schedule, slipping further day by day, and as the Queen's visit was confirmed, the client needed to prepare details of readiness.

Although considerable work was still expected to be outstanding in May, the operator would ensure the site would appear complete.

A cosmetic exercise was to be carried out to enhance the appearance of the terminal on the day, and for all intents and purposes this was done. The oil company would make a huge publicity event on the day and the opening would be a main part of the news and media that evening. Television and national press would be covering the opening from start to finish, and the small newspapers in and around Shetland would have a field day.

The government would maximize the publicity regarding the benefits to the United Kingdom's economy and improving the unemployment situation in Scotland. In another part of Europe, plans were being hatched of a different nature, ones that would send shock waves throughout the globe.

ANOTHER PLACE, ANOTHER TIME

The young bright minds studying at Europe's Universities love debate, the more contrary it is then the better the challenge, in politics the more left wing it is then better is the argument. The young will always debate, argue and demonstrate in that order normally resulting in as much destabilisation as possible to get their point across.

Often the police are involved, violent clashes follow and arrests are made, and by then the original peaceful demonstration have merged with undesirables who are just bent on destruction and violence.

These groups are often professional agitators, they may be linked to a political party or they may be part of organised crime, looking for opportunities.

In Turkey at this time was such a gang and it was organised and legitimate working as the militant arm of a political organisation called 'The National Movement Party.'

This militant arm were called the 'Grey Wolves' legitimate they may have been but at the time they carried political baggage, and many young and ambitious individuals found there way into this organisation.

This semi-political group had been responsible for many murders, exhortation and robberies between 1970 and 1980 with most relating to their far right political beliefs.

This organization had built a notorious reputation and were prepared to sell themselves to the highest bidder.

Its campaign was set up to confront its own country's right wing policies through a legal political party but through daring leadership and greed it progressed further and became more extreme; Its activities soon involved intimidation, violence, and then assassinations.

Growing in stature it integrated with other international crime syndicates, and soon its deeds became seriously extreme.

Such an organization attracts the most daring, notorious and competent people, those who do not mind killing or being killed, a breed alone and one of these was Mehmet Ali Agca. In his late twenties, he was of Turkish origin and like his IRA counterpart Michael O'Byrne nurtured big plans for the future.

At the start of his career Mehmet became the well paid pawn of governments, stabilizing the way forward and clearing any left wing 'debris' that got in his clients' way. Not always siding with the beliefs of his client, it mattered not to Agca because the rewards were good. International crime organizations could always use his type of character, professional, fearless, and ruthless, trained to kill.

In his own country, Turkey, he was driven by politics to rid his country of its leftist tendencies. One particular organization that endorsed this and recruited him for work was The Grey Wolves.

Agca soon became well known in the organization, earning himself a ruthless reputation and he soon became the favourite of their leader Abdullah Cavdarli.

Agca realized that his notoriety in the movement could reap big rewards and he waited patiently for this opportunity. A situation did arise when an outspoken journalist needed to be 'silenced'. His name was Asdi Ipeckci.

Ipeckci was an editor-in-chief of a centre left Turkish newspaper, *Milliyet*. He was an intellectual and a leading activist for human rights.

Istanbul is a civilized city on the Bosphorus, a twenty-mile strip of water that joins the Black and Marmara Seas and separates the old city with the new, wonderful and colourful.

However, it was here where Asdi wrote one of his many articles that seriously offended powerful people, and it was not long before Cavdarli was approached by a Bulgarian agency; he was offered a contract to eliminate Asdi and he accepted.

The Grey Wolves had no hesitation in nominating Agca as the agent to carry out the work and he prepared accordingly.

Leonid Brezhnev, the Soviet leader, was at this time finding it difficult to maintain his Marxist ideals with the Russian people; they wanted to be free of the shackles and join in with the free economy enjoyed by the rest of Europe.

Some powerful members of the Politburo were showing dissent and it was becoming difficult for an old socialist to keep control.

People on the streets of the main Russian cities held demonstrations. It was the mood of the time and people were losing confidence with socialistic values.

The old Russian leader was in decline and he knew that if Russia were to fall to a democratic policy then other countries under Soviet control would follow.

He also was agitated regarding the strength of the solidarity in Poland and Pope John Paul's support of the movement; something needed to be done to curb this growing organization.

Brezhnev, steeped in a Marxist political agenda, knew that he had to diversify people's minds, as Stalin had done before him. He needed a strategy to diversify the down-turn, to manipulate, to create an enemy within.

One tactic by Stalin was to order his own special forces to cause unrest within Russia by setting off explosions in strategic places, with many fatalities. He would then blame them on 'dissidents' or enemies within.

By finding and punishing the perpetrators he became everyone's hero.

Asdi Ipeckci was ruthlessly shot down on his way home by Agca and the hunt was on by the Turkish police for his assassin.

It did not take the Turkish police long before they identified the alleged killer. Their man Mehmet Ali Agca was apprehended and remanded in custody awaiting trial.

The trial was brought to court and Agca awaited his destiny to be decided by the Turkish judicial system.

The phone rang in Cavdarli's office.

"Hello," a girl at The Grey Wolves' office answered.

"Put me through to Abdullah Cavdarli, please. Do not ask questions but do as I say." The instruction was abrupt and chilling and the girl opened a connection to Cavdarli's personal telephone immediately, not wanting to question the caller.

"Yes?"

"There is a call for you, I think Russian or similar," she hesitated.

"Put it through."

"This is Shevchenko, I am speaking from Sofia, you will know me." The caller was assured.

"Yes, what can I do for you, Mr Shevchenko." Cavdarli suspected this could be a proposition.

"We want to give you some business, let us say big business." Shevchenko was baiting his man.

"I am interested in business; tell me what you want," asked Cavdarli.

"Between the 8th and 14th May 1981 Europe will need to be distracted; we want you to do this acting on our behalf."

"Distracted, Mr Shevchenko?"

"We want you to, eh, let us say, eradicate a certain person, a very important person." Shevchenko was leading his man.

"Where?" Cavdarli needed a clue.

"Rome, St Peter's Square. Do we understand ourselves?" Shevchenko had finished.

There was hesitation on the line.

"That could be costly."

"Are you interested?" Shevchenko was blunt.

"Yes."

"Then I will contact you later, with the details." Shevchenko rang off.

Cavdarli sat back in his high-backed chair and closed his eyes. He was in deep thought.

Have the Soviets gone mad? The meeting with O'Byrne was bad enough, and now this; it was going to make one mother of disorder in Europe.

The deal would be lucrative, he knew that; now he needed a figure in his mind to discuss when next speaking with Shevchenko.

But first he needed to get his 'ducks in a row' and the man he wanted to do the deed was now in a Turkish jail.

The organization did not waste time and set the plans in motion to spring its man from jail and move him out of the country immediately to a safe house where he would prepare for the mission in hand.

Cavdarli had started to plan the most audacious assassination of the twentieth century and it needed to succeed with every last detail planned to the second.

To him it was a fantastic financial opportunity for the organization, simply based on the significance of the target.

Cavdarli was in the driving seat when negotiating with the Soviets and drove a hard bargain.

This entailed many telephone conversations with Shevchenko but they finally settled on a figure that was worth just over three million German marks.

Cavdarli spoke on the telephone, his voice droned on in staccato fashion and he wanted nothing to be lost in translation.

"You must be positive, Anton. First confirm the date of the escape, ensure that a passport is available, air tickets and all details for travel in Italy, and make sure that accommodation is in safe houses for him and his Bulgarian counterparts. The Bulgarians will rendezvous with him once he arrives in Rome." After a pause, "I don't know how many exactly, but say four and I will confirm."

There was another pause in the conversation. Cavdarli was struggling with his thoughts, thinking through the details of the plan.

"You may need to gently persuade the guards to assist us."

The voice retorted politely, "In a serious way?"

"As serious as you need, my friend, and as the aristocrat said to the cabman, do not spare the horses."

"What?"

"Do not worry about my humour, just make sure the job is done, and also make sure you keep me informed only of good news."

The phone went dead and Cavdarli gazed out of the window in thought. A short while later he picked up the telephone, "Michael, my good friend, the financing that we spoke about..."

Pause.

"Yes, in American dollars would be fine."

Pause.

"Completion in three weeks is fine."

He put down the phone and then gazing from the window smiled confidently, his thoughts reflecting on his face. *This may put the cat among the pigeons*, he thought and continued to smile.

40

WHERE, HOW AND WHAT

Declan needed to keep up his conscientious attitude to ensure that he would not arouse any suspicions, but it was necessary for him to get out and about on site and find a location for the various charges.

He was also aware it would be necessary to ensure that whatever he did would not be discovered by the security. He slowly walked down to the main gate, turned the bend towards the client offices, and as he did so, tried to visualize the best place for them.

With so many security guards continually scrutinizing the nearby area to the platform it was an immense task ahead of him, but he needed to be positive and clever. It was Declan's decision during the days leading up to the ceremony where these would be located.

The size of the charge would be limited; it needed to be as small as possible to avoid detection, but still be powerful enough to have maximum impact on the platform.

It was necessary that he gather more information if his strategy was to succeed; he wanted to know how many of the opening party would be on the platform. Who would they be? And what positions would the VIPs be in at the appropriate time? He would then need to ascertain the approximate distance between the charges and the target.

It was the detailed intelligence that he needed, and the best place to find this was at the scaffold office. He would however need a good ploy to obtain this information from Archie the scaffold manager.

The office run by the sub-contractor controlled all scaffolding erected and dismantled on the site. It had a vast stock of materials and staff could erect quickly and efficiently on any part of the site. It was their responsibility to erect the platform and staging required for the VIPs at the opening ceremony and also the section of terracing for selected onlookers, mainly management from the oil company offices.

The office was positioned a short distance from the main gate, and set just off the road. The blocks were steel containers stacked two high and converted into offices. As he reached the main gate he felt especially vulnerable, with security now keeping a watch over all of the most critical areas.

The road was almost impassable, with thick mud and water covering the area of transit. Most of the heavy transport had completed its work, and had left the site, but it was still busy as it was used to transport personnel from the gate to their place of work, causing the quagmire that it now was.

Once he reached the gate he turned quickly and headed towards the office. He knew the big scaffolding manager and looked for his cabin.

"Where is Archie's place?" he asked two guys carting scaffold poles.

"He is on the top floor, Paddy, up those steps," and he pointed towards some wooden steps leading to the upper floor.

Big Archie was sitting at his desk and pencil in hand he seemed to be concentrating on where to put his 'x'. The desk was backed up against another, and both were covered in paper and the other chair opposite Archie was empty.

Archie was a big man, his large arms supported by the elbows that were lodged on to the edge of the desk.

His light red hair was protruding under the woolly skullcap, and when he looked up his eyes were almost hidden by thick bushy eyebrows.

He did not recognize Declan at first. "What can I do for you?" His Geordie accent was very prominent.

"Actually, I came to thank you for arranging for the scaffold modifications in the boiler house. As you may remember I couldn't get access for setting the pipework up, and you did it unofficially."

"Oh you are the lad who requested it, are you? Now I remember, and it was a bigger job than I thought."

"I may need some more alterations but will go through the normal procedure so it will be requested officially this time," Declan assured him.

"If you do, mate, then get it in quickly, because I have reduced my workforce and my scaffold pipe store is looking pretty empty. And with the opening ceremony almost upon us, I have some huge priority work to be done, and without men and materials I am going to be fucked."

Declan thought deeply, and tried to select his words carefully. "Then I will get the application in urgently, as I can see that you guys have lots of unexpected work."

Just at this moment another man entered the office dragging his muddy boots behind him. Archie and Declan became quiet and watched the man remove his hard hat and hearing muffs. He then removed his scarf and fur-lined parka coat and slumped into the chair opposite.

He did not wait to be introduced to Declan but glared at Archie.

"They are going to want two fucking platforms and I calculate about 5,000 metres of pipe and clips." He waited a second then went on, "Our bloody office in Glasgow will need to get their fingers out and get the materials shipped like now."

Archie replied, "What are they going to do? Build a football stadium?"

The other man went on, "If the client wants these fancy things for their dignitaries, then they should let us know in plenty of time."

Declan wanted to know the position of the proposed structures, but thought his probing may arouse suspicion.

Archie went on, "This fellow," nodding towards Declan, "wants some scaffold changes in the boiler house, and the last time we went in there, the whole lot needed to be removed as soon as we got it up, then after two bloody days we needed to rebuild it again; took us time," he complained.

Declan interjected politely, "Sorry about that, Archie, but the piping was previously installed the wrong way with the valve flow in a reversed position."

"Orhhh, don't worry, these things happen, and your things are for real, whereas this opening thing by the Queen is all for show and for the oil company's publicity."

"Yes, I read that she was coming, so I suppose there will not be a lot of work done on that day," said Declan. He went on, "Are they building a platform for her and terracing for us bears, as I assume that we will be in on the thing?"

The man went on, "One along the side of the main gate and one up by the terminal isolating valves. This may change, although I would think that the valves will be the main focal point."

Archie suddenly stood up. "That reminds me, I have a bloody meeting about this now, so I must be off, so get that application in, young fellow, as soon as possible, otherwise it may be after May that we can do it."

Declan followed him out of the cabin, but first bidding farewell to the other man.

After the minibus dropped him off at the accommodation that evening Declan missed his dinner, and instead went home to make some decisions. When he entered his room, he inadvertently stood on an envelope addressed to him.

Inside he read the words:

'Have made up the posies.

Will send in the post shortly.'

Declan was relieved because this meant that he would not have to make up the main charges.

The message told him that the IED main charge would be sent through the post, and he would need to add the fuse and detonator, and the hardest part would be to position the charge.

That evening his mind was in turmoil. His orders were to cause as much destruction as possible as a first pass, and should any fatalities occur so be it!

Once detonated, the bomb blast and heat would do the damage, and he decided against improvising any further – enough was enough. No ball bearings, nails or substitute would be used as accessories. However, he would need two devices of about 100 kg each, and also four pipe devices, as he now had decided to position these on the scaffolding using the poles as cover.

He would pack a scaffold tube with ammonia nitrate and detonate it by a simple clock timer.

The charge need only be 2 kg and if carefully positioned would bring down the complete terracing.

The cottage in Brae was no longer part of the plan and this limited him to building a device locally, so he looked for somewhere where he could work in peace and not be detected.

It was difficult to work without a base, so it was important that he find somewhere quickly to make the preparations needed. The main charge would be sent from Ireland, with only the final touches prepared on site. The smaller charges could be prepared much earlier and locally where he stored the materials.

He booked his flight departing from Scatsca the day after the ceremony, but he was also fearful that he might not be able to make it if things turned turtle.

41

COUNTDOWN

APRIL 1981

His last week on leave and away from the island prior to the opening ceremony was stressful for Declan, his mind continually thinking about the things that needed to be done or more importantly those things that he had forgotten to do.

Billy advised him by telephone that there would be two 10 kg packages sent to the box number that Declan had set up with the Brae post office.

The packages were recorded delivery and would arrive two days prior to the date required.

Declan had made up the detonator and tested the timing device, but his main challenge was still selecting a suitable location. Declan had made the 'pipe devices' ready for packing the powder, and he now needed to decide where these would be positioned on the platform. He had not told Billy of his plans and decided that the pipe bombs would, in the long run, be more reliable than the larger devices.

They would be easy to place and the device once packed into the scaffold pole would be more difficult to discover. He was now on his own and made a point of frequent visits to see Archie just to say hello and make sure that his face became familiar with his team.

It seemed to work and he made sure that he knew each of

their names and the topics that they were interested in. Two weeks before the opening day, Declan received a note from Billy saying that he would offer his support up to target date, and noted that he intended to depart from the airport at Sumburgh an hour before the planned time of detonation.

Billy arrived on 24th April and stayed at the Queen's Hotel in Lerwick. The use of a hire car meant an hour's drive to site, but it was not necessary for him to be close to Declan, so he would carry out his task in isolation.

The majority of his work was done in his hotel room whilst at other times he worked in the car, stopping in one of the many lonely country lanes on the islands.

Preparations at the terminal were proceeding for the visit and a massive clean-up was underway. The mud was gone and unwanted sights such as ugly scaffolding removed. It was obvious that Archie's overworked team had been kept busy.

Declan took advantage of his familiarization with the scaffolder personnel, and he made additional clandestine efforts to assess the best places to locate his devices.

It was difficult to justify carrying a bag or backpack without drawing attention from security, so he was forever cautious, always looking for the best and worst times when a lull in security was evident.

Once the scaffold safety tags were appended to each structure, then all other accessories were removed. He had thought that bags of scaffold clips might be left in case of last minute adjustments, and if this was the case he could position the devices in one of these.

Unfortunately he had discovered that for safety reasons the area needed to be totally cleared. He thought of supplying free 'back carry bags' for the scaffolders to wear around site and they could carry all their needs, but this could be taken out of context.

In this way Declan could carry one or leave it with the device somewhere without it being too obvious, especially if each of the men were carrying them also.

What he did notice were some electrical termination boxes close to the stage adjacent to the main gate, and these could be good for placement of the charges. If he could get access to these it might be the perfect place.

Obviously size might be the main factor regarding location of the device, and once this was established he could determine the influence of the blast. He felt that he needed more time to study the situation, but under the circumstances this was not possible, so to make the thing work his assumptions needed to be correct.

Billy wanted to know the final position and the exact time of placement and detonation, and once confirmed he would estimate the size of the device. The pipe bombs were easier to build and manage, and he now knew when and where these had to be placed so he could set the timers twenty-three hours prior to detonation.

The main devices were a problem and he wanted some advice from Billy on the situation. The difficulty was contact without detection, especially with focus now on security.

Declan caught the bus from Brae on Saturday 25th April, just two weeks prior to the Queen's visit, at 12:30 hours bound for Lerwick and a rendezvous with Billy.

Disembarking in the town, he made for the harbour and sat on the wall overlooking the water; it was peaceful and he mused at the huge range of sea birds. Declan thought that some of the birds were so fat that they couldn't even move until further defecation was accomplished, and then they may achieve flight. Looking at the state of the nearby rooftops it seemed to Declan that the birds may well have carried out this procedure many times before.

The fishing boats offloading their catches produced a

potential feast for nearly all species of sea birds, and it seemed that most of these had followed the trawlers from their far off fishing sites, feeding from the entrails of fish that the crewmen had discarded and thrown overboard. These huge gulls often failed to fly with the extra weight, their wings not powerful enough to get lift off.

On this particular day Declan found peace watching the many species of birds, all looking their spectacular best in these serene conditions around the harbour, many of the birds providing an aerodynamic exhibition.

The wind was fresh but not gale force and he had time to identify whether the bird was flapping, twisting or folding its wings, and he marvelled at their antics. He recognized the more common birds, and identified gull-billed tern, kittiwake, great black-backed and common gulls, and others that he could not identify.

It all seemed so peaceful, and he wondered to himself how the situation here would change when all hell was let loose on site. Suddenly the peacefulness was disturbed by the sound of ringing at a nearby public telephone; it must be the call he was waiting for, and he rose quickly to receive the expected call.

"Hello."

He recognized Billy's voice. "I will be down in a few minutes, and I will meet you on the wall adjacent where the boats are berthed. We will not be noticed."

The phone went dead.

"We better be fucking ready on the fifth and the charges placed before the eighth," Billy emphasized these points.

He was not his cool and calculating self and seemed fidgety. He had grown a thin wispy beard and with his eyebrows overgrown, looked a lot older than his years. He was lean and fit, but his body language seemed aged, worn out before his time, shoulders sloping as he spoke to Declan.

"There will be two consignments and I will receive and prepare them both; this way it will be safer."

"Nothing for me?" asked Declan.

"Plenty, as you will need to place the charges, and make sure they go off, then you had better be in a place where no one can find you, because being Irish you will be the first they will go for!"

It was Declan's time to feel nervous, and he paused and thought before answering.

"You're saying that I will not make it."

"Not at all, it will be every man for himself, but there are no safe houses here in Shetland. The best you can do is to set the charge twelve hours before and make sure that you are close to those who can vouch for you when the bang occurs. Look," said Billy, "I will be gone once I have given you the packages so make sure that you think about the consequences and cover yourself."

"OK."

"OK then, I am off. See you in the pub in Brae on Wednesday, and make sure that you pick up the backpack that I leave against my chair, because you will be the first to leave, so do not make your exit obvious."

42

MOVEMENT IN EUROPE

5ᵀᴴ MAY 1981

In the north of Italy, Milan is close to the borders with France. It is the second largest city in Italy, and represents the centre of commercial and financial industries. Both parties representing The Grey Wolves had arrived in Milan after crisscrossing Europe in an attempt to avoid the police and Interpol. The others in the room were of mixed nationality: three Turks, three Bulgarians and an Italian.

Each communicated in either their own language or broken English which seemed universal. The position of the property they rented was excellent, and Mehmet noted it was difficult for passers-by or others in nearby apartments to observe what was going on in the apartment. He found that his team had already arrived at the house and a meal and drink were waiting for him.

In the house, he was introduced to the others who would assist him, and he assumed that all of these were part of the Bulgarian connection selected by Cavdarli. The group consisted of six men and one female, and using broken English, he communicated for about an hour before he decided to retire to his bedroom, exhausted by thinking and speaking in a foreign language.

The group had reached this destination earlier than Agca and prepared the apartment for their short stay, buying food from the local shops. He informed the group that he would not leave the apartment during his stay, and his plan would be discussed and rehearsed over the next few days. He advised them to be careful when outside the apartment and always check for tails each time any of them left or returned to the building.

The next day early in the morning the mood changed, curtains were drawn tightly together, large maps and papers laid out on the kitchen table and the group huddled around Agca. A man of few words, he nevertheless explained the details of the planned assassination and discussed the duties of each of the perpetrators.

Agca's most important accomplice and fellow Turk was a man called Oral Celik, and his principal duty was to detonate a bomb directly after the assassination, a decoy bomb to divert attention and allow Agca and his team to escape.

The Turks were doing most of the talking and it was apparent that the others would play no direct part in the action. The Italian could not speak in English, the Bulgarian interpreting where appropriate, mostly about the plans that the Turks were discussing.

The team would move to Rome and enter St Peter's Square on 10th May and familiarize themselves with the area, and carry out a simple rehearsal.

On 13th May the entire team would again enter St Peter's Square, and take up their positions. Each of them had rehearsed their presence and to avoid suspicion each carried out simple routines of either messing with cameras or writing postcards.

For all intents and purposes they were simple tourists waiting to see and cheer the Pope when he passed by in just a few hours.

Agca's camera bag was next to him but his camera was slung around his neck.

Pope John Paul II entered the square on 13th May 1981.

43

5ᵀᴴ MAY 1981

This was the key day for Declan and his associate Billy Keogh to maintain plans for their assault at the opening ceremony. Their carefully laid plans needed to be finalized by the end of the day, but were to be complicated by extenuating events.

The weather was poor with the sky a dark grey, and the rain fell continuously; it was not heavy but a misty type of rain that clings and makes everything damp. Even after days of cleaning up in readiness for the big day, the roads and buildings looked a mess, the slush being produced by the incessant water.

Declan, fully kitted out in his company wet gear, toured the site evaluating everything in sight but trying to remain inconspicuous. Mud and rain were everywhere and the workers' boots carried the mess into the offices; not a presentable place for a royal walk around. He needed information to share with Billy later that day, and continued to walk and observe the preparations in the rain, but in doing so he also needed to maintain a presence in the boiler house where his company expected him to be working.

At precisely the same time that Declan was walking the muddy roads at the terminal, a very elegant old ship was slowly manoeuvring its way into the harbour in Oslo, Norway ready to anchor as close as it could to the shore.

The Royal Yacht *Britannia* anchored and it began the start

of a five-day royal tour of Norway by Her Majesty Queen Elizabeth and her husband, the Duke of Edinburgh.

As the royal yacht went astern, securing the anchor, Her Royal Highness was having a light lunch with her husband in the ship's restaurant.

"Do you realize, dear, that our anchorage is very close to the wartime resistance museum? If I remember, it is on top of the hill on the headland and part of the Akershus Fortress," the Queen advised her husband. The Duke of Edinburgh smiled as if recalling a distant memory.

"No, my dear, I do remember visiting Oslo before but not the museum." The Queen hesitated for a moment before raising her hand slightly gesturing for help from the steward.

"Please pass me the plate of salmon; it looks absolutely delicious."

They both remained in silence for the rest of the meal, with the exception of requests to the attending stewards.

The Queen suddenly perked up. "Philip, we must prepare ourselves; we are being received by Olav in about two hours, and I would hate to delay any plans."

"Quite so, my dear." He immediately rose to assist his wife.

As the footman held the chair to allow Her Majesty to move away from the table, the Duke suddenly held her arm to steady her as the yacht rolled slightly from side to side.

As the royal couple moved towards the exit, a very smart man of about forty met them in the doorway. He was dressed in a dark blue double-breasted suit, and his hair seemed to be stuck on to his perfectly shaped head.

"Yes, Henry, what is the itinerary for today?"

"Ma'am, the royal barge will come alongside at 14:00 hours and we are to be received half an hour later."

The couple seemed to be taking this in but said nothing, and that seemed to be a cue for Henry to continue.

"King Olav will be at the quayside at 15:00 hours and the ceremony will take about an hour and a quarter."

"That's good, Henry. I am feeling tired so an early night after the ceremony is required."

"Yes Ma'am."

"Oh and Henry, I cannot remember just how soft this carpet is, and I am making hard work to walk on it. I suppose it is a sign of getting old."

"Nonsense Ma'am, it is too plush, but I will help you."

She laughed. "Just a comment, Henry. I can manage, you know."

Henry followed them both out to the ante-room and they slowly disappeared into their respective staterooms.

Henry felt tired and stressed, and wished now for some time to himself, but there was still nearly a week of travelling to do before getting back to England, so he must maintain his enthusiasm until the end of the tour.

It gave him great comfort to think that the next few days were expected to be less stressful than the first few, and with that thought he headed for the kitchens to ensure that all was ready for the afternoon.

It was a time of heightened tensions in Northern Ireland and the long war with the Provisional Irish Republican Army continued remorsefully.

The tensions worsened when on 5th May 1981 Bobby Sands died after a hunger strike in the Maze prison. Sands had volunteered for the Irish Republican Army in 1972, and was soon involved in the Troubles. He was arrested and sentenced to five years for possession of handguns and sent to the Maze prison. He was released in 1976 but soon afterwards was charged with arms offences again and this time sentenced to fourteen years in the Maze.

However, in 1972, William Whitelaw (Britain's Deputy Prime Minister) granted Special Category Status (SCS) for prisoners in the Maze who had been convicted of political related charges. This proved a luxurious concession to the prisoners and they did not hesitate to take full advantage of this status.

This led to discontentment, lack of discipline and a prisoners' revolt finally ending in 1974 when a fire burnt down much of the prison. To re-establish authority the Labour Secretary of State Merlyn Rees phased out the SCS, and the prisoners reluctantly went back to the original system.

When concessions are granted and then withdrawn, the situation always leads to complications and this is what exactly happened in the Maze. The first prisoner to be interned in the new H Block, but retained under the new rules, was a man called Kieran Nugent.

The warders possibly knew that Nugent would refuse to comply, and he enhanced their belief by refusing to wear a prison uniform. Nugent was badly beaten on a number of occasions but remained resolute and continued to go without a uniform, using only a blanket to cover himself. This demonstration by Nugent spiralled in H Block and, as the cells filled up, so did other demonstrations.

More prisoners started to protest in different ways, and soon many were carrying out hunger strikes. Sands was heavily involved and it was clear that he had the mentality to carry out the strike to the bitter end.

The IRA exploited this situation as they were looking for ways to maximize publicity and make the most of a bad decision by the British Government.

On 1st March 1981 the ordeal began and it began five years to the day that SCS had started. A few days later Frank Maguire, the Independent Republican MP for Fermanagh and South Tyrone, died, and left the way open for Sands.

Maguire's function as a Republican MP was solely to keep a Unionist candidate out of Westminster, which he did! During his time in office he only visited Parliament in London a handful of times. This was a great opportunity for the movement and they proposed that Sands run for Parliament.

Bobby Sands MP never took up his seat at Westminster, and after sixty-six days of hunger striking finally succumbed and passed away on 5th May 1981.

It was the ultimate sacrifice for one's belief.

The day that Sands died was also an important day for the IRA at Sullom Voe.

44

BIG DAY

The opening was now a well-publicized event, and was to be made even more so with the news that the Queen would arrive in the Royal Yacht *Britannia*.

It was also known that King Olav of Norway and Prince Philip would accompany her. The transition from the yacht to the terminal quay would be by a royal barge. A car would pick her up at the quayside and take her round to the new engineering support building, where she would disembark and meet up with many of the construction workers.

Inside the building the set-up was indeed fit for a queen and it was here that she would officially open the terminal. Her speech was to take place inside the building and be transmitted to the many workers waiting outside. The plan for the royal party after the speech was to return by car to the accommodation ship SS *Rangitira* for lunch.

Declan was now a very pensive man, and could only now ascertain when the bombs should be detonated. His principal decision regarding detonation was now the timing, and he calculated that the scaffold pipe bomb would be the first when the Queen was inside the building and the main device would be set off just five minutes later.

On Thursday 7th May, just two days before the visit, he met

with Billy who was waiting for the arrival of the first parcel from the mainland. It was addressed to Declan's post office box number and he waited nervously in the background at the Brae post office for both Declan and the parcel.

Declan finally turned up but the two men did not speak, just stared ahead, glaring at one another knowing that this was now the real thing, and they may not come out alive.

Billy was not sure if Declan had heard about Bobby Sands, but before he broached the subject his priority was to prepare the device, then fully enable the charge at a later time.

They took the parcel and walked to Billy's car, making sure that the two of them were as discreet as possible. Billy carefully placed the parcel and contents into his backpack in the boot of the car. He then drove for about twenty minutes and parked in a secluded area in the country.

Billy cursed. "This bloody island is a curse for people like us, because there are not any suitable trees to bloody well get some cover."

"Do you want to go further into the fields?" asked Declan.

"Too obvious; let's stay here to be sure it will be OK."

Billy checked the packages and was surprised to see a seven day timer, which had Declan known before, might have been useful.

"Have yer found a place for the devices, and when are yer setting the time for?" asked Billy.

"I thought that there were two parcels?" asked Declan.

"There was supposed to be, so I expect that the second will arrive tomorrow. I will wait for it and you get the other stuff rigged up. Good luck and I will bring the second parcel to you tomorrow."

"I'll drop you by the bus stop."

Declan visited the site without the package, and decided to review the scaffold structure and at least secure the pipe devices.

However, when he arrived at the engineering support building where the main ceremony was to be held, the area seemed like a railway station in rush hour with so many people.

The scaffold that he needed to access was close to the engineering support building and he was frustrated that he could not get close enough without arousing suspicion. The scaffolders were sticking labels and arrows on the structure that had been erected earlier: No Smoking, No Overloading, Way Out, Steward Control, and so on.

Others were checking the couplings on the joints, and the clips on the platform. Security officers were walking round looking important and electricians were fixing up the sound system and lighting.

He walked up to the area where his first pipe bomb would be secured. He gripped the handrail with both hands and pretended to look at the view.

Instead he glanced down at the joint where his pipe would be appended.

"Yous come for the view, or to book yer place for the show?" A voice bellowed out from behind him and the big man's hand gripped Declan's wrist. Declan turned to see Archie grinning behind him.

"Eh yes, that's about it," said Declan.

"If yous want this place then get here early," said Archie. He added quickly, "Good luck and enjoy. I will see you later, mate," and he jumped down the stairs two at a time.

Damn, expressed Declan to himself, *it seems my cover is blown for placing the pipe devices.* He continued his thought, wondering where he could place the backpack with the main charge without it being discovered. The engineering services building maybe the best place, but that may be too late in the day. Damn it.

He wandered over to the big double doors and saw the type of people working, and after scrutinizing them, thought the best way was to come early on the day, and arrive with the cleaners. That would allow him to set the timer, place the second device and then establish an alibi.

Billy was due away on his flight on the 8th and he himself on the 10th. He would in the meantime place the second device in the power station, with the time set for the Queen's speech. This would be a smaller charge, a decoy to divert attention and cause confusion minutes before his second and main explosion.

The timer would be set only fifteen minutes after the first and the second charge would be more devastating. The Queen, her entourage and the grandstand would all be in disarray and they would be totally unprepared for the second blast.

Declan had the plan and would contact Billy and arrange a location to pick up the second bomb.

Her Majesty the Queen of England was in her third day of the royal tour visiting Norway and Shetland.

The weather was cold and overcast and the Norwegians were looking forward to a long-awaited summer. Many had postponed the spring holiday abroad to get a glimpse of the Queen during her five-day visit to Oslo.

They had always maintained close ties with the UK, and this visit had strengthened the bond between the countries even more. It was at its strongest during the Second World War when the two countries fought side by side against Nazi oppression.

The resistance in Norway during the war was strong and dedicated and the forces made a huge difference to the war effort during the Nazi occupation.

Elizabeth II had not disappointed them and with her natural zest for the big occasion, she put on a regal performance. King Olav and his countrymen were very hospitable, openly celebrating the visit by the United Kingdom's royalty. This incorporated a tour of Oslo, visiting the national theatre, art gallery and opera house. They dined in the opulence of the royal residence and then travelled to visit the exhibitions of Kon Tiki and Viking history on Bygdoy Island.

Norway was about to gain a tremendous boost to the economy with oil and gas becoming a strong player due to the success of exploration in its sector of the North Sea.

On the evening of 7th May whilst Declan and Billy were plotting her destiny, the Queen was at a banquet held in her honour by King Olav. The scene was spectacular and the meal sumptuous with colourful guards of honour, female guests in bright and colourful dresses and the men in elegant evening dress.

It was to be her last formal night before she closed the tour to Norway.

The next night was to be spent on the royal yacht, before it set sail for the Shetland Islands where it would anchor in Voe Sound for breakfast on the morning of 9th May 1981.

45

FRIDAY 8ᵀᴴ MAY 1981

Whilst the Queen prepared to close her tour of Norway, it was to be the penultimate day for Declan, and he still had plenty to do. The day started normally and he went onto the site as if nothing was out of the ordinary. He would check in with his foreman and continue working at the same spot where he had left the day before, in the roof of the power station.

His work card for the next few days was to repair the supports for floodlights and then install supports for another high level circuit; it was an extra to the original design. The timing of this work suited his private situation well: the location was away from the maddening scene of the opening ceremony and it would allow him to set the second device without his superiors bothering him.

He carefully packed the IED, a charge of about 20 lbs of explosive, checked it and set the fuse. The back was lifted carefully onto his shoulders and he set off for the power station.

Approximately one hour later he had placed the charge above the ducting between the trusses of the roof in the power station. The charge was large enough to make a huge noise in the enclosed area and also bring down the section of the roof that was held by the trusses where the charge was placed.

He then quickly completed the work on the additional circuit and lighting and hurried off to collect the second and bigger charge from Billy.

The post office at Brae was busy and Billy was checking Declan's post box every half an hour. The second parcel that was expected on the 6th had not arrived.

The time was 09:05 hours on 9th May and the arrival of the royal party was expected about 11:00 hours. They had agreed to set the first fuse at 12:00 hours and the second ten to fifteen minutes later.

Billy was trying not to look conspicuous. But this was not helped by his loitering and continuous enquiries to the postmistress concerning deliveries. The place was small and it seemed everyone knew each other, with the exception of the nervous Irishman. Impatiently he returned to the hire car and sat watching the post office, hoping against hope that the mail van would arrive with his package.

Just as he was about to get out and make another enquiry, two cars pulled up outside the post office and the driver of each got out and strode into the building.

The men looked like the police, and he now guessed that the package had been intercepted and these were security officers moving in to confront the pick-up person.

He gently started the engine, and without revving, moved slowly away from the post office and slid down the track to the main road.

After about a mile, he stopped at the junction, and hesitated whilst he decided which road he would take. A right turn would take him back to the site and a left turn to Sumburgh and the airport, although both were quite a distance away.

A car hooted behind him in an attempt to persuade him to make a directional decision, and instinctively he turned towards the airport, and drove carefully to catch his flight.

He knew Declan would be waiting for the second device, but had made up his mind to flee as quickly as possible as it was only a matter of time before the security or the police were onto him. The time was now 09.30 hours and he knew Declan would be waiting for contact near to his work phone.

Declan had bypassed his works office expecting to meet Billy with the parcel, and passed the gate and walked out to the water's edge to disguise his presence. He pretended to gaze out at the MV *Britannia* with the Queen on board and the Norwegian Royal Yacht *Norge* carrying the Norwegian King.

There was no sight of Billy so he tried to visualize the situation and the various options open to him. The bottom line was communication. Hoping Billy had not been caught he decided to return to the works office.

"There has been some guy trying to catch you, Declan lad, it must be two or three calls so far," the man, a fitter, called out to Declan as he walked into the office.

"Oh, probably my brother who wants to know what the big deal is here," answered Declan.

Declan was becoming agitated and nervous in case Billy had been picked up. The phone suddenly rang and made him jump.

"Hello, this is Declan."

"The eagle has flown, and the eggs have been found and taken."

"Is that your brother?" The mate came back into the room.

"Yes," said Declan and the line went dead.

Declan knew now that he too needed to make a getaway and the best way would be the night sailing of the ferry from Lerwick to Wick or if he was lucky, to catch the late flight from Sumburgh to Glasgow.

He was booked on the flight on Monday from Scatsca and did not want to bring undue attention to an early departure, as the budgie flights were always fully booked long before the departure day.

Unbeknown to them both, Declan and Billy were on the

road at the same time, although Declan was an hour behind his friend and they had planned different destinations.

He checked the time and it was 10:35 hours, coming close to the royal party arriving at the quayside.

At 11:20 hours Declan paid the taxi driver and headed towards the ferry terminal, but found that he would need to wait until an evening departure scheduled for 21:30 hours, so he would lay low until then.

Billy drove his hired car into the rental bay and pushed the keys through the window to the waiting clerk.

He checked his watch and the time was 11:45 hours.

The next flight was at 14:30 and it was fully booked, so he asked to be 'wait listed'; the next available was the evening flight at 18:00 hrs.

The Queen looked radiant in a peacock blue coat decorated with white buttons on the collar. Her white trilby hat with the peacock blue band matched her coat.

The royal party came ashore from the barge at about 11:00 hours.

After disembarking, she walked along the red carpet to the waiting car that would take her through to the administration building and the short induction.

The sound of the RAF band was trying to overcome the noise being produced from the harbour, the sound of a flotilla of ships all with sirens blaring.

Both Declan and Billy, in different places, checked the time; it was 11:15 and the charge for the one remaining bomb was set for 12:00 hours. They were both now aware that once the bomb exploded, security at the airport may close down everything and they may need to change plans.

The Queen, unaware of any peripheral activity, continued her visit normally and after completing introductions in the administration centre walked outside onto the platform to receive a rapturous welcome.

As she walked to the car for a tour of the site, she was greeted by hundreds of adoring oil workers, all of them wanting to see and greet her. After the tour of the site, she spoke with some of the men along the barriers near to her path, and then made her way to the engineering services building where the inauguration ceremony was to take place.

The time was 11:45 hours.

The building interior was decked out in red and blue carpeting. Seven RAF trumpeters greeted the Queen as she entered the building and made her way to the staged area where her speech was to be made. Both the British and Norwegian national anthems were played before she started her speech.

The time was 11:58 hours.

As her crisp and clear voice echoed through the speakers, and spoke about the economy, the oil delivery intentions and the excellent work carried out at the terminal, there was a significant noise, more than a thud and less than a bang but enough for all inside the building to notice with alarm.

The Queen continued her speech as though nothing had happened, but the noise alerted the security and a group of them left the building to investigate.

"What the hell was that?" one of the men asked a policeman standing outside the building.

"It seemed to come from the power station. There are four of our men on the case."

The security men followed, both now shouting into the short-wave radio transmitters. The Queen, still unperturbed, had finished her speech and was now unveiling the plaque. Within minutes the whole party left the building and made its way to the MV *Rangatira* where a luncheon was laid out in royal fashion.

At the Brae post office the clerk had received a large package, addressed to a D. McBride. It was possibly the name of the Irishman asking for a package yesterday.

He was busy and tracing this McBride person may take too much time. He called to an assistant, a short girl with brown wispy hair who was sorting letters on the window bench.

"Mary, will yer please re-address this package 'return to sender' and let's get on with our work." The clerk was busy and agitated. Mary looked at the clock to see whether she had time to do this request or leave it for the morning.

"OK, Mr Sherborn, I will do it now and they will pick it up in the morning."

"No, Mary, keep it for two days and if he does not come for it by then, send it back to where it came from."

"What do you think that it is, because it is bloody heavy," asked the sorter.

"None of our business, so let's send it back and it will be their problem."

At the power station the six officers were examining some damage where the device had exploded and were relieved to find that the roof was still in place, so they moved tentatively around other areas checking for other devices.

"It was superficial damage and the charge small," said one of the men as he was speaking into his radio set.

"Could it have caused more damage if it had been placed more strategically?" said the voice.

"A bigger charge, positioned in the right place may have shut down the turbines," answered the guard.

A voice on the radio announced, "The PIRA have claimed responsibility for a bomb."

The radio went dead then the voice came out loudly, "Please check the power station thoroughly and report back."

"We will check other areas including all outgoing transport, planes and the ferry."

Unbeknown to the royal party, a huge manhunt was underway at the terminal, and over the length and breadth of the island.

Security teams were searching the terminal for other devices, whilst police combed the whole of the Shetland Islands looking for the perpetrators.

Billy opened his eyes and checked his watch; it was 17:00 hours. His waiting for the previous plane was in vain, but he had managed to book onto the next flight, but still had an hour to wait.

"Excuse me, sir, are you waiting to depart the Shetland Islands?"

"Who wants to know?" Billy was suspicious.

He turned his head backwards as to see the person that he was addressing.

"PC McHugh," answered the policeman. "And this lady is PC Wilson."

"Your passport please," asked the policeman.

Lerwick police were at every airport and ferry terminal in the Shetland Islands. Many had dog support, each sniffing the individuals waiting to board.

The ferry was at the quayside but not a car or person had yet boarded and it was now nearly an hour behind schedule.

Declan was in the cafeteria and could see what was going on. He walked over to a group of police talking close to where he was sitting.

"What's going on, officers?" he asked brashly, trying to sound confident.

"It is a routine search," said one of the officers.

"Oh, I thought for a minute the ferry was cancelled." He

tried to hide his Irish accent. He smiled and turned towards the queue waiting to board. The barrier lifted and the front car slowly moved up the ramp.

At the same time the passenger barrier was lifted and the passengers moved forward, but the search and questions by the police slowed things down.

"I have been on this bloody island three months, and I can't get off to my house." The man next to him was very irritable. Declan did not say a word but shuffled on behind the person in front, in his mind rehearsing what he would say to the police who were checking credentials.

Where is Barney now? he thought.

He decided not to look the officers in the eye when the questions came.

46

A VERY TOUGH AND RIGHTEOUS PERSON

Pope John Paul II, the leader of over 600 million Catholics around the world, was invested as Pope two years earlier in 1979. He had the distinction of being the first Polish Pope, and the first non-Italian to hold this office in over 450 years.

An avid traveller, unafraid to walk in public, and always ready to integrate with others whatever their religion, he was a man of the people. The Pope, brave and proud, stood in his open carriage, driving through St Peter's Square, blessing his followers and his smile reached out to nearly every heart present.

It was the start of his weekly general audience at St Peter's; he thought this would be no different to the other days. One of the people in his path was not a follower nor was he looking for a blessing, and his cold grey eyes followed the approaching Holy Father and cold and calculating he waited.

His name was Mehmet Ali Agca and in an instant he shocked the world.

Suddenly and without warning the assailant struck. Amidst thousands of his followers they heard what they thought was impossible, four loud retorts, and Pope John Paul II fell to the ground.

Security guards were on the scene in seconds, some looking for the source, whilst others attended their fallen leader. People were screaming and running in all directions fearing more shots. It was pandemonium but the chaos may have been worse if Agca's accomplice Oral Celik had detonated the bomb that his team had planned, but in the mayhem he too panicked and ran from the scene, discarding his gun and device detonator as he ran away.

Agca also panicked after the shooting and was quickly overcome by security agents and carried towards a waiting police van that sped him away.

Oral Celik, fortunately for onlookers, failed his leader. He was soon picked up by the security forces and later sent for trial.

The Bulgarians, at a distance from the action, waited to offer support but they too fled; two of them were apprehended later to face charges with Agca and Celik.

His Holiness unbelievably survived the shooting and continued to serve his followers until 2005. Pope John Paul II, among all his other endeavours, is well remembered for his efforts in supporting solidarity and an end to communism and the Soviet Union.

It is bizarre that the erosion of communist power and the fall of the Berlin Wall occurred in 1989 just a few years after the first assassination attempt on the Pope.

THE BROKER
WEST LONDON, 14TH MAY 1981

Hyde Park is magnificent in the spring and this particular year was no different. People rid of the winter were eagerly looking forward to a warm summer.

The Serpentine was still, apart from the frolicking of some ducks in the clear waters. Some boats were on the Serpentine; a few of the oarsmen were struggling and laughing at their own ineptitude, whilst others were trying desperately to impress female passengers.

It was the month of young love and together with the trees and flowers it would expect to flourish and bloom as time passed by.

Alongside the park runs the Bayswater Road and the noise was a contrast to the tranquillity of the park with traffic bustling along, the drivers impatient to reach their destinations. Close to the road just opposite Lancaster Gate tube station the curtains of a hotel room were held; a man inside was looking out and at the same time talking on the telephone.

"I am trying to talk with Comrade Dmitry. He works at your organization and I need to talk with him; it is important and urgent and he will understand." He seemed agitated.

"No, I only speak English, and yes he works at your department; please connect me. What do you mean he does not exist? Of course he…" The line went dead.

He continued to stare from the window, and after just a few minutes picked up the phone again and dialled a Dublin number.

"I would like to speak with Danny O'Rierdan." After a pause, "Yes, that is the correct spelling and I have spoken with him on a number of occasions. He has moved? I did not know. OK, please give me his contact number. Thank you." He put the telephone on the handset.

The bellboy knocked and delivered a bulk of newspapers that the man had ordered.

Hastily the man called O'Byrne spread the papers over the hotel floor and scanned each one quickly.

Across the floor of the room were spread a selection of English daily newspapers; the dates covered an eight-day time period from 5th May until 13th May 1981.

O'Byrne checked the deaths column, and this showed

Bobby Sands' passing. No deaths or injuries were reported at the opening ceremony.

On 13th May he noted the headlines that Pope John Paul II had been shot and was in a serious condition in hospital in Rome.

Then on closer inspection in one of the newspapers, as almost a footnote, he noted that a bomb had exploded in the power station at Sullom Voe, but he seemed annoyed when he scanned the report: 'There were no injuries, although some damage was done to the roof and the power station boilers.'

He noted that MI5 had levelled blame on the operator for not supplying adequate security to prevent such a threat. He stopped reading any further and he felt despondent. It seemed that he had failed in delivering what he had promised.

O'Byrne recoiled. He was not happy and sat on the settee to ponder his situation. He was troubled; the situation did not look good.

Dmitry was not responding, nor was O'Rierdan, and he felt that a call to Cavdarli might not be appropriate at this time.

He considered contacting Maria but thought that she would not be in the loop at this stage and anyway, he was not sure where she was at this time.

The situation appeared unsatisfactory, both operations that he had brokered were not successful, and he was the man who promised the Bulgarians he would deliver.

He also assumed that MI5 would have him under surveillance, but he was not sure who else.

Both the Irish and the Bulgarians would be dangerous and show no mercy if they did find him. He needed to obtain a new identity and lay low somewhere but now he felt alone, with no allies or organizations to turn to.

The phone rang. "Hello."

"This is DO, your friend from Dublin," informed the caller.

"DO, who is… OK, I remember, Dennis," answered O'Byrne.

"Where are you?" DO asked.

"London, just off the Bayswater Road," informed O'Byrne.

"Two days from now I will meet you on the Embankment, the third bench along from Westminster Bridge, and we can discuss your next assignment, at say eight in the evening." The line went dead.

Two days later the weather had changed and O'Byrne found a chill wind as he left the tube station and walked towards the bridge. Crossing the road he turned left along the Embankment to locate the third bench. He was ten minutes early.

He felt totally alone with nowhere to go and was now waiting for an Irish dissident who probably could not be trusted, but he had no alternative. Finding the exact bench was confusing; the co-ordinates given to him were not exact, so he lent against the river wall where he could look along the walkway and see anyone approaching.

He waited over an hour and no one closely resembling O'Rierdan appeared. Feeling nervous he approached the road to hail a taxi. He did not have to wait long as a black Mercedes with an illuminated sign on its roof, City Taxis, pulled up.

"To Lancaster Gate, driver." He decided to return to the hotel.

The car accelerated but quickly slowed for the lights at the bridge; in a second the back door opened and a large person squeezed in the door. O'Byrne tried to intercept him but the man was too heavy and sank into the seat next to him.

With a thick Russian accent the man introduced himself.

"Eh, sorry for the impromptu entrance, Mr O'Byrne, but it is necessary."

O'Byrne was nervous, and his mind in disarray.

The car drove along the Fulham Palace Road and turned towards Chelsea Bridge.

"My name is Sergei; you may know who I am, and if you do not, your good friend Maria Andropov reports to me. Because of the failure of the recent events you must now depart the country quickly so we have taken the liberty of arranging your flight to Sofia where you will start a new life, at least in the short term."

"But what if I have other plans, Mr, eh, Sergei?"

"We cannot be responsible for 'other' plans. Please do as I say."

"When and what time is the flight?"

AZERBAIJAN, 17ᵀᴴ MAY

Three days later in Baku, Azerbaijan, Maria Andropov was strolling along the promenade alongside the banks of the oil-rich Caspian Sea.

It was busy but not crowded and allowed her to enjoy the warmer breeze after a long and cold winter. Her partner Boris Golov was slightly shorter than Maria and had an oversized waistline.

"What are your aspirations for the future, Maria?"

"Comrade Golov, I intend to support the party, and to pursue my career at home in Moscow."

"I will help you, comrade, but I intend also to pursue my own position within the security organization." Golov was boasting.

"What are your own plans, comrade?" Maria enquired.

"I have applied and it seems been accepted to transfer to the KGB operations in Poland to support the party there." There was a pause. "Join me, comrade; we will make a good partnership." He was now wooing her.

"Comrade, that is a generous offer. Please allow me time to consider."

"Of course, and by the way, have you heard of the news

regarding your old acquaintance from the IRA? You remember O'Byrne." He glanced at her to evaluate her reaction.

"Nothing," Maria answered, "but should I?" she asked.

"He apparently travelled to Sofia for a meeting with our Bulgarian comrades, but became ill, I think a heart attack, and died early this morning."

Maria was stunned into silence but quickly composed herself.

"He was young but was discredited after the fiasco in the Shetlands, and then Rome, I believe." She seemed matter of fact.

They turned and started the long walk back to their hotel.

47

A BOARDING HOUSE IN LANCASTER – CUMBRIA

15TH MAY 1981

Lancaster was alive with colour after a hard winter and the buds and flowers were nearly a month late. The daffodils had come and gone and bluebells brightened up the town's green areas.

Mrs O'Shea was particularly busy with her boarding house full with a mixture of clients. Some were young couples experiencing the spring and young love whilst others were single men on some business or another.

Her partner Sean was busy washing down the outside steps that fronted the house and spoke with every passer-by who would listen to him. As he was about to clear away his broom and apparatus his eye caught the postman struggling with a large brown paper bag.

"Hello George," his Irish accent bringing a smile to the postman's face. "Is that for me?" he said and opened his hand to the postman.

"Yes, Sean, but it is a return to sender and I will need a signature," the postman said with a growing authority. He produced his receipt book and Sean signed his name.

"Thank you for that," said Sean as he turned with the parcel and made for the door of the bed and breakfast. As he mounted the steps and entered the hall his wife was saying her farewells to two clients leaving the premises.

"It's for you, dear," he said and handed her the parcel.

"I've never sent a parcel this big for many a year." Puzzled, she opened it to find a mixture of fertilizer.

"That is fertilizer," advised Sean and whispered that it may be from one of the boys.

She looked annoyed, and staring straight at Sean held her reply for a moment.

"It's probably one of the boys who has been up to mischief. You may need to dump it as soon as possible." Sean seemed more concerned for the 'boys' than the contents.

"Not at all," said Mrs O'Shea and she picked up the telephone. "Inspector Keanen please."

She waited as the operator put her through to another extension.

"Inspector, this is Mrs O'Shea, from the South Sea guest house. I would like to report a package that I have received. It is a return to sender but I have no idea who sent it in the first place. May I suggest that you come to pick it up?"

She waited whilst the inspector asked his questions.

"There is no name of the sender, only my address and the contents. I think it is police business."

She waited and listened.

"I am not sure what the contents consist of, but you need to see them."

The reply was short.

"That's fine, sir," her voice was clipped. "I will be waiting."

She put the phone down, and glaring at her partner said, "Do not even go there, Sean, we know nothing and know nobody." Her face was hard. "If some fool of a person wanted to post a package from here, and not inform us it is their business. You know the situation and right now we want no part of it. Do you understand?"

"Yes," answered Sean obediently.